STRANGE FRUIT

A NOTE ON THE AUTHOR

DS Sheridan was born in the magical land of Maebh and Graineuaille, where the mists swirl down from the slopes of Croagh Patrick. As befits someone born near the site of the pre-Christian battle of Moytura, she is intuitive and hypersensitive.

She lives in London where she works as a psychotherapist.

Fintan Walsh

STRANGE FRUIT

D. S. SHERIDAN

POOLBEG

First published 1993 by
Poolbeg Press Ltd
Knocksedan House,
Swords, Co Dublin, Ireland

A catalogue record for this book is available from the British Library.

Poolbeg Press receives financial assistance from
The Arts Council/An Chomhairle Ealaíon, Dublin

ISBN 1 85371 268 X

Cover artwork by Jordan Baseman
Cover design by Pomphrey Associates
Set by Mac Book Limited in Stone 10/15
Printed by The Guernsey Press Limited,
Vale, Guernsey, Channel Islands

To those I love and cherish who have given me their unstinting support and love (S.G.I.M.D.C.)

My heart has followed all my days
something I cannot name.

Don Marquis

PROLOGUE

Dublin

How long have I been here?

I cannot count the days.

How long have I been curled nose to knees, a question-mark on your cold bed? My head is buried in the dent in the pillow where your head has been. A drummer pounds a tattoo on the skin stretched taut over the top of my head. My temples throb with the force of each beat. He demands an answer to the question:

Why? Why? Why?

In the cavern behind my closed eyelids, your face flares, the face of a child, wonderstruck, behind a sparkler on bonfire night. Incandescent now, you glow even brighter than the day you climbed on to the roof to surprise the foolish crow that had built her nest on the chimney-pot.

The smoke from the fire huffed and puffed its way up the chimney, then down again and out into the sitting room. I heard your laugh as I fell over the chair, knocked the fern, then yanked the brass curtain-rail down on my head, before I flung myself, choking, across the window-sill.

Your smile broke through the smoke, radiant as the sun when an aeroplane rises above the clouds. You squatted in the cobbled laneway, back to the wall, elbows on knees...I glimpsed no shadow world behind that open smile.

A musty odour fills the room. It seeps through the walls, drops from the ceiling. It hovers over the bed. I press my face into the pillow and take small panting breaths. I try to block the fumes that threaten to suffocate me.

Through soft duckling down and limp linen pillowcase your perfume takes me by surprise. Dabbed on temples with long jasmine-tipped fingers, touched behind ears. Camomile and peaches rinsed through shining hair...

I know that you're here.

But this is foolish. Only primitive, untrained minds believe in ghosts.

Yet the house vibrates with your energy. Your presence fills the room with such force, there is hardly space for me. My mind seesaws between conscious rational thoughts and powerful irrational feelings that feather my nerves and keep my senses standing to attention.

I squeeze my eyes tight. I know that the morning light, which creeps across the floor, will suddenly recoil, startled to encounter your opaque figure standing motionless beside my bed, your hair a dark cloud about your shoulders, your eyes beseeching me for the help I cannot give.

What is it you want from me?

Is there something you have left undone?

CHAPTER ONE

12 March, Notting Hill

"I've won the pools. Let's run away."

I smiled, teasing the boy as he handed me the envelope. Black leather mimicked matchstick body, boots buckled, sleeves fringed, anaemic face, acne and white eyelashes.

The pale eyes avoided mine, eyes made vacant by the exaggerated semicircular movement of jaw, and soft sucking noise of chewing-gum lobbed between palate and tongue.

The drum laid down the beat on his Walkman. Cymbals exploded at the end of the eight-bar phrase. Verse, verse, chorus. Verse, verse, chorus.

I slid my finger underneath the flap and eased the envelope open without tearing it.

Rosemary B died tragically at Church Close.

I glanced back at the boy, a question in my eyes, but he was insulated from intrusion, numbed by chewing-gum and hard rock.

His movements became languid, dreamlike. He mimed a scene in slow motion, as he picked up the helmet from the seat of the bike, placed it on his head, covered the left ear, then the right, protected the earphones with long spatulate fingers, tied the strap underneath his chin and pulled the visor down to protect his face.

Rosemary B died tragically...

The distant thud of drums struck at my head with small hammers, then rose to a climax. Big drum lead-in. Repeat chorus until fade. I searched in my pockets for the pieces of silver to send him on his way, but when I found them he had gone. A dark angel of death, powerful, on a black chariot.

I sat on my bed and read the words. I reread them, counted them. I searched them for something overlooked. I willed the invisible ink to reveal itself, to unmask the macabre joke.

Seven ordinary words lay quiet on the buff-coloured page.

Rosemary B died tragically at Church Close.

Your name.

My house.

You in my house.

Dead.

I stared at the walls of my bedroom as though I had never seen them before. In the paint-shop, blobs of vivid colour had dived recklessly into a whirlpool of white. They swirled and churned, then lengthened into ribbons of more delicate hues until this cochineal emerged, triumphant.

In the street, the ring-handle of the heavy can bit into my fingers. A child stumbled against me and knocked it out of my hand. It burst open on the pedestrian crossing. At first the paint spread in a leisurely way. It swallowed the black stripe, then the white. It devoured the studs and the letters that said "Look Right." It gathered speed as it snaked down the zigzags. Angry eyes changed colour under orange lights. A coating of Flamingo drenched the tyres of all the cars that passed by. The street blushed with shame until the rain came and washed it away.

A grin of delight lit up your face as it flashed before my mind. In a heart-shaped face, under dark wedges of eyebrows, eyes the colour of conkers spilled over with laughter. A cleft on the chin softened a confident, intelligent face.

What deathblow could my house have dealt you?

You were young, strong…

Did you fall down the stairs, did your clothes catch fire? Did you surprise an intruder, who hit out at you in panic?

My thoughts flew back to a spring day in Dublin. I wandered through wet streets, past a row of terraced houses. A stone plaque caught my attention. Shamrock ringed the words:

Bernard Shaw, author of many plays, was
born in this house, 26 July 1856.

As I meandered towards the canal, I spotted a tiny

house that nestled in a cobbled laneway. It had shuttered windows, and a crooked chimney, as if a small child's chubby hand had drawn it with fat crayons.

The roof with its missing slates ogled the inscrutable sky with a lopsided grin. A broken gutter hung over a strip of verdigris, where the slow water dripped. Weeds trailed in small cracks. Lower down, where the doorstep met the cobblestones, tufts of nettles and dandelions grew.

Dirt streaked the windows. Old lace curtains hung frayed and twisted. On the window-ledge, a geranium had expired in a brass plant-holder. I pressed a fat brown paint bubble with my thumb, and watched as it bulged back to life.

I listened, then lifted the tarnished door-knocker and tapped three times. No one answered. Very gently, I pushed open the letterbox and peered inside.

The room was tiny. Brown linoleum covered the floor. Coffee-coloured wallpaper hung from the walls. Rickety stairs disappeared drunkenly above eye-level. From the mantelpiece, two white china dogs with black snouts and raised eyebrows stared at the smoke-blackened ceiling.

I was enchanted. It looked like a discarded doll's house. I bought a newspaper and some chocolate in the local shop.

"Nice day."

"Indeed it is, thank God."

"It's quiet around here."

"It is that. Too quiet sometimes."

"Do you happen to know who owns that small, empty house in Church Close?"

"Ah, poor Mrs Reilly. God rest her. A grand woman."

"And the house?"

"It's up for sale this good while, but it's in a terrible state. It's falling down."

"Who's selling it? Is there an agent?"

"Indeed there is. Go back on to the main road. Turn right. He's there on the corner. Don't tell me you're thinking of buying it?"

"Who knows?"

I found the agent. He was delighted to show the house to me. It was indeed falling down, and had a strong smell of damp and decay, but no one or nothing could have dissuaded me. Driven by something I couldn't have named, I borrowed and begged.

In record time, I became the proud owner of the small fairytale house.

I put my name on a waiting list for a telephone, then threw myself into restoring the house. With the help of builders, carpenters and plumbers, I coaxed it back to life. I watched as they measured, sawed and hammered, listened as they whistled and joked. Little by little, it began to take shape until it looked like a gingerbread house, all ready to eat.

The walls were coated in white icing, chocolate buttons replaced the missing slates, liquorice the chimney, and a slab of marzipan the front door.

Inside, it became a house of crystallised ginger and rose-coloured Turkish delight.

I searched auction rooms, rummaged through second-hand shops, picked up treasures in junk-shops. I drove in the rain at rush-hour in a car loaded with lamps and chairs, a small sofa balanced precariously on the roof.

At last, it was finished.

The kitchen was minute. It had an electric cooker, a refrigerator and a stainless-steel sink. One careless movement could send dishes, pots and pans crashing from shelves and hooks on to the floor.

In the sitting room, wooden beams supported the ceiling. There were book-filled shelves, a table, the small sofa, chintz curtains and some chairs. A portrait of George Bernard Shaw hung in the place of honour over the fireplace.

The workmen had removed the old shambling staircase. They had opened up the pitch-black hole that had been a cupboard underneath.

New wooden stairs brought the space to life. Two strong vertical posts supported a bannister bolted into them. Fifteen open steps reached upwards. They turned to the left and led to a fairytale room of sweet dreams. The ceiling sloped over a brass bed, a hand-painted chest of drawers and a white wicker chair.

In the tiny bathroom, seashells I had bought on a holiday abroad held the soap in delicate ivory palms. Old-fashioned scent bottles filled the shelves.

Early one morning I went to the market. I placed a vase of sweet pea on a small table in the triangle underneath the stairs, and filled every corner with lilac, freesia and roses. I lit the fire.

It was perfect.

ii

"What a sweet little house."

You passed by as I turned the key in the lock one day, a smiling stranger, dressed in jeans and a blue sweatshirt.

"Do you live here?"

"Sometimes."

"It's so pretty."

"Come and have a look."

I could never resist a combination of spontaneity and enthusiasm.

"I'd love to."

Wide smile, gap between front teeth, a sprinkle of freckles. I opened the door.

"It's beautiful. It's like a doll's house."

"That's what I thought."

You darted about, touched wood, books, ornaments.

"Would you like to look upstairs?"

"Oh yes. Please."

A headlong dash, two stairs at a time. Laughing, I went to put the kettle on. Over the sound of running water, I could hear your quick, light footsteps.

You came downstairs slowly.

"It's magic. Absolute magic. I love it."

"So do I."

"Why don't you live here all the time? If it were mine, I couldn't bear to leave it."

"I have to work."

"Why don't you let me rent it when you're not here?"

I laughed.

"I'm serious. I'm looking for somewhere to live. I'd look after it for you. I'd leave whenever you wanted me to."

I poured two cups of tea.

"But I don't even know you."

"I know, but take my name and telephone number. Please. If I thought I could live here for a month, even for a week, I'd wait forever."

"Let's see how it goes."

"Promise me you won't forget."

"I promise."

When you left, I laughed out loud. You had reminded me of myself.

iii

I glanced around at the rows of figures hunched over desks in the insurance office, and rang the bell. A young man looked up. He started to uncoil his long body. Bony ankles and wrists protruded from his suit, as if he had grown several inches after he'd bought it.

"Can I help you?"

"I'd like to insure my house. I'll be away. It's going to be empty."

"How long will you be away?"

"I don't know."

"They won't insure an empty house."

"Bloody hell."

"I'm really sorry. It's the risk, you see. Squatters and all that."

Dark eyelashes fringed guileless eyes. A tuft of hair sprouted in the cleft between lower lip and chin, an unexpected salute to Tom Waits, the Blues, and ghosts of Saturday nights. Born with such a stain, he would have worried and fretted, focused his anxious adolescent attention on it, until he forced his parents to take out a second mortgage to have it removed.

"Could you get someone to stay there while you're away."

"I don't know. I could try, I suppose."

"Come back if you have any luck."

A slow smile nudged the tiny hedgehog that lolled above his chin. Aroused from its torpor it protested, then stretched and yawned.

I found the scrap of paper you'd given me. It was on the mantelpiece under the china dog's front paw.

I dialled the number. "I wondered if you'd found somewhere to live."

"No." One syllable, two notes, the first low, cautious, the second high-pitched, excited.

"I'm going to be away..."

"Are you going to let me have it? Are you?"

"Yes, if you would like it."

"I'm so happy. I've never been so happy. I'll take care of it. I'll guard it with my life."

iv

The cheep of sparrows in the trees outside brought me back to the present. I glanced through the window. The sky had not darkened. The earth had not trembled. There was no sounding of trumpets. There was not even a whisper to verify that your young life had ended, and mine would never be the same again.

I fell asleep and you slipped into my dream. It was a dream of locked rooms and silent screams, of mirrors that showed no reflection. A shadow stalked me through deserted streets. It flitted past me and beckoned. As it turned its head, your face looked at me. I tried to run, but my feet remained rooted to the spot.

Shocked awake, I sat up and wiped cold perspiration from my face. I picked up a book from the top of the pile by my bed.

With a single drop of ink for a mirror, the Egyptian sorcerer undertakes to reveal to any chance comer, far-reaching visions of the past.

I read the sentence over and over, then put the book down and picked up another.

Like distant music, these words that he had written years before were borne towards him from the past.

I stared at the words until they blurred, then closed my eyes.

This time, the recurring nightmare jolted me into action. Year after year, as far back as I could remember, this dream had tormented me. Imprisoned in a concrete room, deep beneath the earth, I beat against the walls to escape. I searched for doors, but there were no doors. I tore at the concrete to find a window, but there were no windows. I was trapped forever, because I had been careless. I had lost or forgotten the one vital thing that would release me.

When I awoke, I found I had ransacked the bedroom, stripped the bed, scattered books, pulled out drawers and emptied them on to the floor, searching for the lost thing.

I stepped over a mound of bedclothes and went to make a cup of tea. I glanced at the kitchen clock. Three o'clock in the morning. I filled the kettle, and wrapped my hands around it as it throbbed to the boil.

A thought trembled in a dark burrow deep inside my brain. I ignored it. It refused to go away.

I concentrated on the second hand of the clock as it jerked around the circle. The more I tried to block it, the more agitated it became, until a cold nose reached in and expertly ferreted it out.

Somehow, alone and vulnerable in the middle of the night, I knew what had happened to you. Don't ask me how. It was a sixth sense, a gut feeling, something I could not explain. I argued with myself, repeated jokes, put-downs.

> *You women and your intuitions...if you're so clever, tell us the winner of the Gold Cup at Cheltenham...we try to educate them to be reasonable, logical. It's a waste of time and money.*

But nothing could shake the feeling. There had been no accident. No intruder had struck you down. I knew without doubt that you yourself had been both victim and executioner. With a fearful triple stroke, you killed, you were killed, and you died...

And the backdrop you chose to stage your drama was my beloved doll's house in the cobbled laneway.

CHAPTER TWO

"I'm going to end it all. I'm going to end it all in the river."

The little girl looked up from where she squatted by the cot. They would waken Stella. Her doll had just gone to sleep. Blonde, curling hair covered the pillowcase. She tucked the eiderdown in on each side. It was sprinkled with primroses, buttercups and forget-me-nots.

Rock-a-bye baby on the tree-top
When the wind blows the cradle will rock.

Her daddy had his hand on the brass doorknob. His face was very white.

"Do what you like. It makes no difference to me."

Her mother held her head back to one side, all stiff. Her cheeks were pink and her eyes shone like the buttons on Stella's black patent shoes.

The child sat back on her heels. She curled herself up, until she was as tiny as a fairy, then leaned forward and pressed the place where her nose started into the side of the cot. As she peeped out, her eyelashes tickled her first fingers.

Her daddy turned the knob, pulled the door open and walked out. Her mother followed. She listened to the cross voices until they died down. Then she began to rock back and forth with the cradle:

Rock-a-bye baby on the tree-top
When the wind blows the cradle will rock.

She pressed her lips together tight, but before she could stop them, two hot tears escaped. They slid down her cheeks, splashed on to her wrist, and slid up her arm.

"Daddy, Daddy don't go away."

ii

The river ran right through the middle of the town. Sometimes it was green and made a splashy sound, and the fishermen caught speckled salmon. One day, Mr McIntyre caught a *lamper-eel* (lamprey). It wiggled and wriggled in the middle of the road and all the people came to look at it. It was long and straight, with one nostril and a huge mouth, like Mrs Kelly's vacuum cleaner that she got from America, for sucking the dust out of corners.

Its eyes were covered with skin and it had rows of horny orange and yellow teeth that didn't go up and down like salmon's teeth. They went in and out. It was horrible.

One of the big boys pushed Joe Duffy and he nearly fell on top of it. All the children screamed and ran away. They hid in case he picked it up by the tail and chased them with it. Michael Murphy climbed a tree, but he fell out of it with a thump because he got such a fright.

The small girl ran to her daddy. He lifted her on to his shoulders, so that she was taller than anyone in the whole world. She could reach up and touch the sky. She wasn't afraid then. She knew she was safe.

Sometimes, when it rained and rained, the river got dark. It burst its banks and flooded the fields, and the trees grew up out of the water. It made hardly any noise then. It swished under the bridge and bubbled into whirly, gurgly dimples. When it reached the "mad falls," it roared and burst into the white froth the men in the pub wipe off their moustaches.

Further down, near the place where the big boys played football on Sundays, the river had no bottom. Mrs Walshe said that a horse and cart fell into it once and were never seen again. Mrs Duffy told her that they had gone to Australia.

One day during the floods (it was the day Mr Duffy ran over the two frogs—it was a mistake; he didn't mean to) a cow fell in and got drowned.

The water swept it down under the bridge. It got caught in the weir near the school. All winter it bobbed up and down in the water. When she lay in bed at night, she prayed for it. She imagined the *lamper-eels*, swishing their tails as they sucked at it under the water, hoovering the brown hair off with their huge open mouths, leaving only the white blubber.

There was something else she didn't want to think about, so she whispered it to the sleeping Stella.

Sometimes, when people have puppies they don't want...they put them in a bag with a heavy stone and drop it in the river...tiny floppy puppies that are all warm and snuggly, knitted together with their eyes closed...

She always knew when there were new puppies, and went to visit them. Tinker O'Hara and Spot Murphy had tiny little sausage-puppies, but when she went to see Patch Jordan, the puppies weren't there.

"They've all gone to heaven," Mrs Jordan said. She was suffering from fatness and had flour on her arms.

Patch ran around the yard. She searched for the puppies and whimpered. The child felt the cold nose nudging her hand, *on account of* she was asking for help to look for them. She put her arm around the small dog. Then Mr Jordan came out of the house, and told her to go home like a good girl.

She reached over to pull the eiderdown up until it covered Stella's rosebud mouth.

When the bough breaks, the cradle will fall,
Down will come baby, cradle and all.

Without a sound, she got to her feet and tiptoed upstairs. She picked up the teddy-bear with the fat tummy and the turned-in leg. She washed him, combed his hair and hung him up to dry...

To wash the bad things away.
To make everything all right.

CHAPTER THREE

Next morning, at the airport, I bought a ticket for a flight to Dublin. The girl behind the desk tapped the computer, waited, then tapped again.

"Smoking, non-smoking?"

"I don't mind."

"Which would you prefer?"

"Whichever..."

"Window seat, aisle seat?"

"It doesn't matter."

A look of irritation skimmed her flawless face. "It would make it easier if you'd say which you prefer."

I tried to focus on her face, but she was at the wrong end of the telescope.

"It doesn't matter. It really doesn't matter."

Late now, hurry, hurry. As I stepped through the security check, the metal on my belt triggered off the alarm. Everyone turned to look.

Run, run. I dodged left, right and left again to squeeze past a short, square woman. She controlled the corridor, determined that no one would pass, fat arms thrust out by her sides, each footstep planted firmly in the earth. Men with briefcases hurried towards us from the opposite direction. Workmen stood around dressed in overalls.

I ran up the steps, nodded at the smiling crew, found my seat, folded my raincoat, pushed it into the compartment overhead, banged it shut, then sat down and fastened my seatbelt. I longed for a cigarette, but the red light showed "No Smoking" and I was seated in the aisle seat, non-smoking section.

The throbbing inside my head beat to the slow rhythm of the muzak:

Dead, dead tragically dead
Dead, dead tragically dead

The tape dipped and slowed as if the musicians waded underwater. Undeterred, they slurped on.

Dead, dead tragically dead
And who but my Lady Greensleeves.

The pilot's voice sounded. "Welcome on board. Fifty-minute flight. Temperature three degrees. Raining in Dublin."

Always raining in Dublin, grey Celtic mist, seven years beneath the sea before the Day of Judgement.

"Height of 30,000 feet, route Slough, Birmingham, Wales, the Irish Sea."

We swept up, up and away, through the clouds. The sun blinded me for an instant, reflected off the wing. We dipped to the right.

How...

How did you do it?

The engines hummed, flaps retracted, smell of diesel, a baby slept on his mother's lap. Of course, sleeping pills, that's what they do, pills bring dreamless sleep, dissolve shadows, dissipate pain.

The baby awoke. He stiffened in protest, displayed two new front teeth as he screamed and threw his rattle on to the floor. A smiling hostess bent to retrieve it. She wore a red-and-white scarf, knotted at the side.

Red on white...

The bathroom. Red liquid oozed from ugly gashes, as your life's blood snaked towards the stopper, to begin its slow descent to the earth. Spiders scattered in horrified flight.

Stop. No more. Push the thoughts away. I watched blue smoke spiral upwards from smokers' seats, listened to rich coughs from nicotine-stained lungs, counted nineteen ribs of hair, carefully distributed across the bald head in front of me, "parted above the waist." A joke from somewhere.

"We are now beginning our descent. Please fasten your seatbelts."

Bump through the black clouds. Rattling and rolling, the lurching Trident slammed into the runway with a thud. Trays crashed out of stainless steel drawers. Someone cried out, "Jesus, save us."

A woman across the aisle turned to look at me, eyes bulged with terror, mouth twisted. The fat woman who would not allow me to pass had encountered a situation she could not control.

The compartment overhead sprang open. Belongings scattered. My dark green raincoat uncoiled and dropped. Caught somehow, it hung motionless before my eyes, a king cobra poised to strike. Then it started to move.

The metronome of my eyes followed its wide creaking sweeps, "tick, tock, tick, tock." Inside my head, a snake-charmer's flute piped a tune:

Southern trees bear a strange fruit
Blood on the leaves and blood at the root
Black bodies swinging in the southern breeze
Strange fruit hanging from the poplar trees.

A blinding spotlight pinpointed a hitherto untouched section of my brain. I felt sick, suddenly, violently, physically sick. I searched in the pocket behind the airline magazine for the waterproof bag.

At that moment, I knew what you had done.

CHAPTER FOUR

"I'm going to make a cot for the Commander-in-Chief."

Daddy always called her the Commander-in-Chief. She didn't know why really, but she liked it because it was special. Once he promised, she knew he would do it. He never forgot like grown-ups did sometimes.

One day he came home with wood that had a nice warm smell. "It's called deal," he said.

They went into the shed. Stella opened her eyes, then closed them again and said "Mama" when he put her down on the table to measure her.

"Gosh, she's growing," Daddy said. "She must be eating her porridge."

The child sat down on the ground, with her back to the wall and her legs stretched out straight. Daddy put Stella on her lap and Dicky snuggled up beside them.

They all watched while he measured and sawed and hammered. He did not speak while he worked, but sometimes he turned to look at them and smiled his big smile. She could see eleven teeth. She knew it was eleven, because when she sat on his lap, she tapped each tooth with her finger and they counted them together. He wore glasses and his eyes were brown. They were the colour of toffees...not the hard toffees, the soft ones. She could fit nearly three fingers into the dimple on his chin.

His hair was dark. When he washed it, it was straight at first, then when he shook his head, it ran into lots and lots of little curls. He parted it, not on the side you bless yourself but on the other side, where his heart went "thump, thump, thumpety, thump" when she put her head against it. He smelt of tobacco and a soft leathery smell, like the inside of a car.

He whistled while he worked. Sometimes, he did not look at them, but he tapped a tune on the wood with his fingers. She always knew what it was: "Somewhere Over the Rainbow" or "Run, Rabbit, Run, Rabbit, Run, Run, Run" or "D'ye Ken John Peel?"

He measured the wood and marked it with a pencil. Then he sawed it into pieces. He put some of them flat on the table for Stella to lie on, then he made four posts, one for each corner of the cot. He fitted a rail into holes in the posts. Then he put an umbrella overhead, and *roundy things* on the bottom, so that it could rock and put her to sleep without too much trouble.

Each time he shaved the wood, it ran into long blonde curls. She picked them up and put a cluster on top of Stella's head. She hung some from Dicky's ears with hair clips. He shook his head and sneezed and tried to take them off with his paw. But he didn't mind really.

The rest she put on her own short hair. She felt very grown-up when the long ringlets sprang up and down on her shoulders. They brushed against her cheeks when she rolled her head from side to side. Corkscrews yo-yoed in front of her face when she nodded.

She tossed her head and flicked the ringlets behind her shoulders with the back of her fingers, and made a face like Mary Browne did when Jim Hardy went into the shop to talk to her.

Then they all sat in a row as quiet as mice. They watched until the cot was finished. Then they put Stella into it and covered her with the eiderdown that Santa Claus brought, and put the lace pillow underneath her head.

CHAPTER FIVE

I telephoned some friends from the airport. They invited me to stay, came to meet me, welcomed, fed, made me comfortable, talked, told stories, made jokes. I tried to respond, but could not fight my way through the blur of unfocused faces and distant voices.

I wanted to talk to someone who knew you, but we had no friends in common. I was a name scribbled in your address-book, no more. Too late for your funeral, I missed the only opportunity to stand shoulder to shoulder with the people who cared about you, to hear them say your name, to ask the questions I needed to ask, and to gain some comfort from a shared sorrow.

In a state of shock, I avoided my own house. It dominated my thoughts. I pushed it out of my mind. Still, it loomed over me. Aimless day followed aimless day. Agitated night stalked agitated night.

I trailed around the newspaper offices, stood in queues under harsh strip-lighting, feigned nonchalance as I pored over ragged piles of print. I scrutinised morning papers, evening papers, early editions, late editions. I searched only for your name.

I found nothing. Not one line reported this bolt from the blue. No paragraph explained your sudden violent explosion of anger.

Each morning, before the light came, I walked down to the sea. I spent day after day in the shadow of the Martello Tower. The March wind bit into me, salt spray showered over me, the rhythm of the waves drew me down into the dark places.

Once every twelve hours, the tide surged from the open sea into the bay. White horses dashed cartons and wooden boxes against the rocks. They swirled over the supermarket trolley that lay twisted on its side. Dribbles of lacy foam raced unevenly on to the sand, getting bolder each time. They chased the pied wagtails as they rushed and stopped, rushed and stopped, in their search for insects, tails bobbing at each pause.

The polished bodies of the seals glistened. They dragged themselves along the rocks, wriggled, rolled on to their backs, flipped their flippers, touched cold noses with their tails, dived off, disappeared, reappeared. When I clapped my hands, they turned to look at me, vaudeville entertainers, hungry for applause, with their starched whiskers and their huge moist eyes.

The cormorants arranged themselves like pins in a bowling alley, then scattered and dived off the rocks. In the water, they pushed forward with powerful movements of webbed feet, wings pressed close to their sides. They crammed their crops with fish before rising to the surface.

They gulped them down and opened their wings to dry. With tail-feathers spread, white spring thigh-patches showing, they became phoenix rising from the waves.

One day, as I stared into the sea, a shooting star scorched through the darkness of my mind. Have the house blessed. Why had I not thought of it? Have the blessing done on Easter Sunday, time of resurrection, forgiveness, hope. Memories of childhood rushed back. What could be more appropriate?

The fact that I had long before shed the cloak of stultifying Catholicism for less demanding agnosticism escaped me at that point. I sprang to my feet, turned my back on the cold, threatening sea.

The lapsed Catholic returning to the fold.

The prodigal son; prepare the fatted calf.

I hesitated outside the church. A short distance away, the small house crouched in the laneway, alone and unloved.

"Cheer up."

A drinker's foolish face paused in mid-whistle. I zoomed in on beetroot eyes, a nose pitted with open pores. Wisps of cotton wool plugged a shaving cut caused by a trembling hand.

"Cheer up. It may never happen."

I waited for a surge of anger to explode in my chest. Cocky, his hands in his pockets, he resumed his carefree whistle which he decorated with trills and tremolos.

And more, much more than this
I did it my way.

A vibrato as wide as his staggering stride shored up his temporary swaggering ego.

I crossed the road and turned into the deserted side-street. I heard only the sound of my own footsteps as I passed the row of terraced houses. Invisible reins guided me. Spurs urged me on. The house reached out to me.

In the window of the corner shop, a cat dozed among the chocolate bars. A kitten poised on hind legs swiped at the string of the blind, then held the acorn between her paws. A whiff of Indian spices mingled with the familiar smoky smell.

A black dog crossed in front of me, the product of a random union. He gripped a chicken bone between strong teeth, a sharp bone that would splinter and puncture his stomach.

"Drop it, boy. Drop it."

He stood quite still. Short hair bristled on the back of his neck. He glared straight ahead. His eyes lightened in colour, legs stiffened. He curled his lip back to expose gums and teeth. I knew he would be quick and very strong.

I crossed to the other side of the street. I could see the house, a side view of shutters, window-ledge, doorstep and downspout. Slow dragging footsteps felt the uneven cobblestones. My heart hammered. The knot inside me tightened.

Dust covered the door and the windows. Weeds grew again in the cracks. I bent down to pick a rogue dandelion, which had turned into an early puffball. Bitter milk spilled in my palm. I blew at the down. The long reddish seeds quivered. One, two. Three o'clock.

The house had slipped back on its hunkers, small, defenceless, full of secrets and unshed tears. I pressed my head against the door and closed my eyes. Then, very gently, I pushed open the letterbox and peered inside. I could feel my eyelashes tickle my first fingers as I glimpsed the open stairs and the upturned chair. I let go. It snapped shut.

The black dog appeared. The chicken bone had not improved his temper. He walked purposefully towards me, and without taking his eyes off my face, threw back his head and began to bark.

I glanced at my watch. It was three o'clock. Three o'clock on a Friday and I lurked like a criminal outside my own house.

Without warning, the realisation kicked me in the stomach. It was Good Friday. Three o'clock on Good Friday.

And behold, the curtains of the temple were torn in two from top to bottom, the earth quaked, the rocks were split, the tombs opened and the bodies of many holy men rose from the dead.

The long-forgotten words surged through my mind. My heart strained to escape from its cage.

Appalled at the cruelty of the coincidence, I blindly retraced my steps to the church. Inside, I sat down as the congregation prepared to leave.

Purple covers draped the statues. Only the crucifix remained uncovered. Transfixed, I stared at the slender young body that hung from the cross, head slumped forward, soft honey eyes glazed and lifeless.

CHAPTER SIX

There was great excitement on the day that the woman arrived from America. She wore a blue raincoat, and had white shoes and a hairnet. She smelt of mushrooms.

"Aren't you going to open your present?"

The little girl started to ease the paper off the huge parcel. She was shy because everyone was watching.

At first she saw the roof of the doll's house, then the upstairs windows, and downstairs. When she opened the front door, the sitting room had tiny furniture, and the kitchen had a doll's tea-set and a range. Upstairs there was a bedroom, with a wardrobe and a bed and a chest of drawers.

"It's lovely."

She forgot about being shy. She even forgot about being afraid when grown-ups talked in special voices, in case she didn't understand what they were saying.

"It's just lovely."

There was another box too, a long narrow box. She

opened it. Inside a doll lay sleeping. Long eyelashes curled on her rosy cheeks. Frilly skirts billowed out when she picked her up. Wavy hair bounced around her shoulders. The child gave a little skip.

"Aren't you going to say thank you to Mrs Riley?"

"Thank you very, very much, Mrs Riley."

The boys hung around, holding their own presents. They pretended they weren't watching, but she knew they were peeping out of the corner of their eyes.

While everyone was talking and having tea, one of the boys looked straight at her and nodded his head. She knew immediately what she had to do.

She glanced around to see that no one was looking, picked up the box and the doll, and slipped out of the room.

Once outside, they all ran as fast as they could. They only stopped to grab shovels out of the garden shed. Serious and silent, they gathered under the apple tree.

The small girl laid the box on the ground, and put the doll in. The big eyes closed, and the eyelashes settled on the chubby cheeks. She arranged her dress nicely, and spread the hair on her shoulders, and gave her a little kiss to say "goodbye." She put the lid on the box.

The boys started to dig a hole with shovels that were much bigger than themselves. She reached up to pick an apple. The birds had got there first. It had turned brown where they had pecked at it with their sharp beaks. She bit around the marks.

She felt very happy as she listened to the sound of the shovels digging the hole. This was the dolls' graveyard.

Her brothers buried all her dolls underneath the apple trees. She grew up believing that this was what dolls were for.

Only Stella escaped. Santa forgot to put her into a box. They got so used to having her around that they completely forgot to bury her.

She stood under the same tree where the dogs hung by their hind legs after they had eaten poison. The men forced soapy water down their throats to make them sick. Their long bodies stretched out almost to the ground, but they never got sick. They died, all full up with suds.

It started to rain a little bit. She stuck out her tongue to catch the cool raindrops, and curled it at the tip.

The shovels scratched against a stone.

"It's Hell," one of the boys shouted.

She looked down and saw the flat slab of stone.

"It's the roof of Hell."

Their faces turned white.

"Run, run."

They yelled with fright as they dropped the shovels. They fell over the box. With a gurgle, the doll fell into the hole. Her head cracked against the roof of Hell. Her dress fell over her head and showed all her frilly petticoats.

"Run, run."

They ran for their lives. Nettles stung her legs, and blackberry brambles tore her dress.

"Don't let him catch you."

The thought of the Devil climbing out of the hole and chasing them made them run even faster. One of the boys fell and cut his knees. No one stopped to help him.

That evening, the children sat at the kitchen table and did their homework, even though it was only Friday.

"What's wrong? You're all very quiet," Daddy said. Nobody answered. They were listening for the knock on the front door, either Satan himself or the priest and nuns to tell about them. They didn't dare to catch one anothers' eyes.

Hissing whispers broke the silence.

"It was all your fault."

"No it wasn't."

"Yes it was."

"I'll tell about you."

"I'll tell Mammy."

Small mouths tightened. Pencils dug into ruled copy-books.

That night she lay awake, terrified at what they had done. To let the Devil out of Hell must be the worst sin of all. It was worse than chasing Mrs Higgins's hens, or eating all the raisins. It was worse than drinking the baby's gripewater and filling the bottle with water.

It was worse than asking for a big ice-cream, and paying for it with a flat stone covered with silver paper. It was even worse than taking the guards' boat on summer days, when they all piled in to go to the island where the men made poteen. Water gushed through a hole in the bottom. While the big boys rowed, the small children baled out with cups and tins they kept hidden in the woods.

She imagined Satan roaming the countryside in the dark, popping up in the wood behind the trees, with all his Works and Pomps, drinking in the pubs, and foxtrotting on cloven hooves at the dance in the Town Hall.

She watched for dark shadows at the bedroom window, and listened to her heart in case it stopped beating. She froze at the thought of what lay in the blackness under the bed.

"Mammy, Mammy, I'm dying. My heart has stopped."

She nearly fainted when her brother shrieked at the top of his voice. He threw back the bedclothes and ran down the stairs to the quiet voices and the warm fire.

She pulled the blanket over her head and squeezed her eyes tight. The wind huffed and puffed at the trees outside. It rattled the windows. She shivered. She knew it was her fault that the doll lay in the dark under the apple tree. She was to blame because she had run away and left her sprawled on the roof of Hell, frightened and alone.

Racked with guilt, she wanted to talk to the picture of Jesus on the wall, but she suddenly remembered the Relic. She had cut the paper off the back of the frame and taken the small silver square from behind the glass. She only wanted to know what His garment looked like. She had wrapped it up again, disappointed that the small piece of cloth was so ordinary. It wasn't a white robe like the one He was wearing in the picture. She put it back behind the glass, but all the same, she had been waiting to be struck down.

"I'll be good," she whispered.

"I'll be good for ever and ever."

"I'll never do bad things again if you make him go back to Hell."

She squeezed her eyes tight and put her fingers in her ears.

"And please don't tell the Holy Ghost about the Relic," she added as an agonised afterthought.

CHAPTER SEVEN

Were you here when the tall priest came to bless the house? I was too preoccupied to notice you then. I stood in the doorway, frightened to step inside.

"Come in."

"I'm fine here, thank you."

Laughing, he looked at me, and shook his head from side to side. "I hope you don't believe in ghosts, or expect me to cast out devils."

Perhaps it was a joke. Maybe he wanted me to laugh. He'd spent most of his life as a missionary in the Philippines. We'd talked about primitive people and superstition on our way from the presbytery.

"They drink Holy Water," he had said. "Poison themselves to keep the devils out."

He took a small bottle of Holy Water from an inside pocket. "What do you want me to say?"

I almost said, "Bless the house, the chalice that offered the sacrifice of a young life. Help it to forgive its own treachery. Release her. Let her spirit soar away from her torment."

But that would be embarrassing. Too flowery. There are never words to say the really important things. So I smiled my easy smile. "Whatever you say to bless a house. You're the professional."

He took a purple stole from the back pocket of his black corduroy trousers, kissed it and slipped it over his head. He ducked and stood, stooped, underneath the stairs.

"In nomine Patris, et Filii, et Spiritui Sancti..."

His practical farmer's hands held a prayerbook. The leather cover curled back at the edges. His left thumbnail was blackened, a blow from a hammer, perhaps. Clerical grey eyes matched cable-stitch sweater. They used to wear vestments and smell of mothballs. Now they dress in jeans and play the guitar. They beguile smiling brown children with "Danny Boy," while they themselves long for the song of the lark and the smell of damp earth.

"O God, Who sent Your Son down from Heaven..."

The house looked forlorn, chair overturned, wood splintered on one step of the open stairs, ashes and a half-burnt log in the grate, ashes on the rug. A yellow film covered pictures and mirrors. Cushions pressed flat into the corners of the sofa. Curtains hung at half-mast.

"Bless those who live in this house..."

On my left, I looked into a tangle of once graceful foliage, now twisted in upon itself. The fern, one of the most ancient plants, five million years old, withered from lack of care and love. No coiled party blow-out buds ready to spring, frilled, crested and fringed, with a feather at the tip.

"Pour Your blessings on Your servants..."

The chart on the kitchen wall dangled by one corner:

Whatever can go wrong, will go wrong.
The light at the end of the tunnel is the light of the oncoming train.

I used to think it was funny. A seaside landlady's notice would have been more appropriate:

No smoking.
No drinking.
No visitors after nine o'clock.
Animals not allowed.
Suicide not allowed on these premises.
If you wish to kill yourself, please do so elsewhere.

"In the name of Your Son..."

The picture of George Bernard Shaw hung crooked over the fireplace, long beard, long face, big ears, high forehead. The eyes followed us around the room, impish, compassionate, watching the priest, watching me. Dear Mr Shaw, what have you seen with your kind, shrewd eyes?

This house was built before he was born. Did you know that? I used to wonder if the serious young boy, dressed in knickerbockers and holland tunic, ever ran away from his "frightful and loveless" home to come here in search of love.

"In nomine Patris, et Filii, et Spiritui Sancti..."

Father, Son and Spirit. What does it mean?

I tried to imagine you as a newborn star, streaking home to some splendour in the sky. Nothing came. So...what are we?

Are we merely plants that live for a time, then die? Or are there harps and clouds and fires that burn forever?

Dear Mr Shaw, is there a God?

Cool drops rained on my cheeks, as the priest sprinkled the room with Holy Water. Did you scream for help when he slipped the stole from his shoulders, kissed it, rolled it up and put it in his pocket? Did your cry fall on deaf ears?

In silence we walked through the door. I banged it shut. Absorbed in my thoughts, it never occurred to me that we left you behind, to mull over your last angry action in this world.

CHAPTER EIGHT

The small girl sat on her hunkers, like Jack Horner, behind the bed. Her heart went "thump, thump, thump." She hugged Stella tight. She held her very still in case she said "Mama" and gave everybody a big fright.

Her mother was going to die. She lay on the bed, but she wasn't all hunched up like she was when she was only sick. She lay flat under the pink eiderdown. Her mouth was open, because her head had fallen down on the pillow with a big bump. Her arms lay by her sides. She was too weak to lift them.

"Willie, Willie."

She groaned loud groans, like Mr Henry's cow Bluebell did when the fairies brought Daisy, the little wet calf. Daisy was all wobbly and couldn't stand up, and Bluebell mooed because she was very very worried. It wasn't the little moos cows do with their mouths closed when they are waiting to go home to be milked. She opened her mouth and the sound came from right down inside her and got louder and louder, then died away.

"Willie, Willie."

You see, Uncle William did something bad. She didn't really know what it was, but her mother was very, very upset, because it disgraced the family. She could not have one of her *tatters* (rages) because he was in the pub. He did not even *know* that she was going to die *on account of* he was bad.

"He'll hear about it from Mrs Murphy *proberly,*" she whispered to Stella. Mrs Murphy held the record for getting news fast from the top of the town to the bottom.

Uncle William wore a hat and his fingers were all brown. Sometimes he staggered a little bit. She never, ever, sat on his knee, but he let her light his cigarettes. He talked about cars, and horses and greyhounds. She did not really like greyhounds *on account of* they drank warm milk and raw eggs for their breakfast, and they couldn't play "chase the ball" or "shake hands" like Dicky.

Daddy and Uncle David stood beside the bed, one on each side. Their faces were as white as sheets.

"Ellen, Ellen, don't go," Daddy said.

"I'm getting the doctor," said Uncle David.

"No. No doctors. It's too late for doctors," she whispered. She was on her last legs.

Then Daddy and Uncle David bumped into one another at the door, because they were crying and couldn't see properly. They went downstairs to get tea and some brandy.

When they had gone, the mother sat up in bed to tidy it a bit, and to make the pillows nice and fluffy, so that it would be comfortable to die in.

As she turned her head, she caught sight of the quiet little girl with the frightened face. Her eyes got all big and her mouth fell open. She pulled the side of her face down and dropped her eyelid in a big wink, like how Stella's eye gets stuck when she's had her face washed and her eyelashes are wet...or how the blind on Carabine's shop window falls down all crooked on half-day.

The small girl *squdged* her face up and stuck her thumb into her mouth. She pressed it tight against the soft place behind her front teeth. Then she closed her eyes and began to suck.

Her mother was often very sick, well, nearly every Sunday she had a stroke or a terrible headache. The curtains were always drawn to keep the sun out, in case it made her worse.

"After all I've done. Nobody cares what happens to me."

She had a small green bottle of smelling-salts beside the bed. It smelt like the hairdressers, when Mrs O'Reilly had a perm. She sniffed it, as the child crept into the room. She could see the hunch in the bed and the shape of the wardrobe.

"Mammy, Miss Jones said I was the best girl in school."

"Go away from me. My life isn't worth living. I've spent the best years of my life..."

Her voice sounded like the special voices people used in the church to say the Rosary, so that God would know they were very, very good, and wouldn't fly into a *tatter* and send them all to Hell.

Her mother didn't take her clothes off when she was sick on Sundays, in case visitors came and she had to jump up to entertain them, and send out for Battenburg cake or Thompson's gâteau.

Downstairs, everybody was very quiet and made signs if they wanted to say something. If the bedroom door shut by mistake, her mother had to crawl out of bed to open it, so they would know when she was dead.

CHAPTER NINE

I met your parents for the first time on Easter Sunday. I leafed through the directory until I found the number, then telephoned and asked if I could call.

I paused outside the door, took a deep breath, then rang the bell. A young man answered. Without a word, I followed him into a room.

Two figures sat in armchairs. They were propped up, their backs to the light, as if the energy had drained from their bodies. I looked into the hollows where their eyes had been, and touched cold, limp hands.

"I'm so sorry."

From the shadows of your mother's grief-ravaged face, your face looked back at me, but the edges were softened, the bright light dimmed, the wilfulness tamed.

"I'm so very sorry."

Outside, the shadowed grass was starched white, until the pale wand of the sun touched each blade and sprinkled it with diamonds. Daffodils spread their yellow petticoats, wanton, under budding trees.

In a corner of the window, a spider's web sparkled with dewdrops, the orb divided into sections, a spoked wheel, with crossbars that ran from spoke to spoke. For a moment, it trembled as an insect struggled, ensnared in the delicate silk. Then all was still.

Why spring? Why did it have to be spring?

You trudged through the dark tunnel of winter. Did you not see the snowdrops rise like miniature snow-geese, their wings outstretched, heads straining towards the sky? You must have noticed when they bowed in homage to the newborn year.

How could you turn your back on blossoming and chirping, on hedges full of thrushes' nests, on warm speckled eggs bursting with future song? What calamity could force you to lie where the poisonous yew trees shed their pollen, when you could sit upon a bank instead and close your hands over soft clumps of primroses?

"Rosemary really loved your house."

The cadence of the speech was an echo of your voice. Knocked off balance, I remained silent. Then a torrent of questions swept through my mind. What happened? Why did she do it? Did she leave a letter? Why did you allow it? Where have you buried her? Where is her grave?

But people don't talk like that.

A dumb actor, I stood in the wings. No one had written any lines for me. My role should have been the landlady, corseted and stern, brandishing a sheaf of lists. protected by inventories. But I had no props. Instead, the resonance of the chord you touched drew me back to childhood. I had learnt to smile when I was most afraid. So I smiled my brave, bright smile.

"Yes, it is a nice house."

And that was that. The opportunity slipped away.

"Would you like something to drink?"

"Yes, please."

"What would you like?"

I searched my mind. No inspiration came. "Anything. I don't mind."

We smiled at one another, smiles that went on too long, while we racked our brains for a safe topic of conversation.

"Such a pretty colour."

I looked down at myself. I wore green, the colour of hope. The legs, arms and torso, banded and zipped, seemed to belong to someone else. I examined the pockets at the hips and knees. My eyes focused on the gold signature, upside-down on the breast pocket. Every morning, I picked this garment from the floor, straightened it, stepped into it, zipped it up and forgot about it.

I felt the shoulder pads swell until they seemed to fill the room. My eyes caught sight of the green suede boots with the gold heels. Shame surged through me. Flippant, out of place, I had intruded on grief dressed like Cruella de Ville.

"I bought it in Munich," I said, as though that would make it all right.

In the silence that followed, someone placed a gin and tonic in my hand. I prattled on. "It was during the

Festival. The hotels were full. There wasn't a room available anywhere. A hotel manager told me that his mother sometimes kept guests at her apartment, so I stayed with her."

Still no one spoke. I gulped a mouthful of the bitter drink. Suddenly, with suicidal folly, I leapt upon the stage and filled the dangerous silences with chatter.

"In the morning, she laid the table with silver and starched linen. There were dishes of sardines, tomatoes and rolled slices of cooked ham, and a cake like a Christmas cake, without the icing. I said I never eat breakfast, but she looked so crestfallen I sat down. I took a sardine, a tomato and a slice of ham.

"She looked like an Earth mother, maybe lived on a farm once, with a husband, children and geese to feed. Now she was alone and lonely.

"'Good?'

"'Good.'

"'More?'

"'No, thank you.'

"'But it is for you.'

"I selected the smallest sardine, a slice of ham and half a tomato. I tried to distract her attention as I pushed it around, searching for a hiding-place in the pattern on the plate. I placed the tomato in the centre of a red rose, the ham on a pink carnation, and divided the sardine between a bunch of grapes and a blue bird that flew past. The pale eyes watched every move until I was forced to swallow it all.

"'Now, cake.' Her face shone.

"'No, no thank you. Not eat cake. Never eat cake, not even at Christmas.'

"'But I make it for you. This *Morgen*. Five o'clock.' She tapped the agitated watch that heaved on her mutinous bosom.

"'Well, only a small slice. A taste.'

"I remembered boarding school when pockets bulged with cold cabbage. Now I wore a sleeveless dress with no pockets. She settled into smiling folds of flesh, to watch my performance.

"'You like?'

"'Delicious.'

"'I make more coffee.'

"She disappeared into the kitchen. I grabbed the slice of cake and ran to the lavatory inside the front door. Locked inside, I dropped it into the bowl and flushed. When the deluge stopped, it stared balefully back at me. I looked around in desperation. New apartment block, no window, no hiding-place. I flushed again. The cake swirled around, then settled down in spite of wind and wave, indestructible, every currant, nut and candied peel intact. I crossed my fingers and flushed again. Still it remained, a battleship impregnable in a storm.

"Flushed with guilt, I wrapped it in tissue paper and hid it in my bra. As I walked through the door, I saw her, seated at the table, knife in hand, poised to cut another slice.

"'More cake?'"

The high-pitched voice, that seemed to come from somewhere outside me, *Leacocked* its way to the end of the story. Suddenly the room exploded with laughter.

For a moment, everyone had forgotten. I had slipped on the childhood cloak of clown, to blot out the reality.

No need for questions. No need for answers.

I finished the drink and stood up. We smiled at one another and shook hands, relieved.

As I left, a woman arrived. Dressed in black, face white, a family friend, with the right to mourn. She had known you better and longer than I. My only connection with your tragedy was that it either began or ended in my house.

Now I lie here, helpless as a foetus on your cold bed. You stand over me, your unswerving attention fixed on me. This is not an ending. This is a beginning. What do you want?

What could you possibly want? Whatever it is, I know that for me, the play has only just begun.

ii

I had to get away.

I bolted for the airport and caught a flight back to London. But wherever I went, the memories went too. Your face never left me.

I chain-smoked until I felt physically ill. I willed the nicotine to cloud my tired brain. I swallowed lethal amounts of alcohol, as I tried to drown myself in forgetfulness. But ice-cold reality held me firmly in its grip. The blissful escape of drunkenness eluded me.

Horrific dreams interrupted moments of sleep. Night

after night, I fled from the locked room of my recurring nightmare. I awoke in the lift, on the stairs, in the street.

Each time I returned to the chaos I had created. I had ripped the sheets off the bed, yanked out drawers, emptied their contents on the floor, in the frantic search for the lost thing that would release me.

Except on Sundays. Then no dream disturbed my vigil. All night long, I stared at the ceiling, until it was time to stand up, to face another impossible day.

It was on just such a night that you had struggled with despair and lost.

CHAPTER TEN

"Who is the best child in the class?"

Nurse Kelly smiled at the children. She was wearing her blue dress with the white collar. A big watch hung into her pocket, from a chain pinned to her dress.

"Who's going to be first? I wonder if the little girls are braver than the boys?"

Nobody moved.

"You won't feel it. It's only a little jab."

They sat up straight, arms folded.

"You can tell your mammies and daddies how good you were at school today."

Michael O'Regan's face *squdged* up and he started to cry. Tom Doyle joined in. The rest of the class sucked their thumbs.

"I can't believe it. Not even one..."

The small girl stood up. She walked to the top of the class. Nurse Kelly picked her up and put her sitting on her lap. She felt soft, like Granny's sofa with the feather cushions, not like Daddy or Uncle David.

"This is the bravest girl," the nurse said.

The child nodded. "I'm not afraid of spiders even," she said.

"Not afraid of spiders?" said Nurse Kelly.

"I lift them up on my copybook and put them on the window-sill."

"But they have an awful lot of eyes," Nurse Kelly said.

"And they have lots of legs, too—more than seven. Daddy said when one leg falls off, another grows in its place."

The nurse rubbed something cold on the child's arm. "That sounds like a good idea. Now close your eyes. I know you won't cry."

ii

She never cried. Ever. Even when the door banged and *squdged* her hand. The bendy knuckles started to bleed, and the small dimples turned blue. She hid it in her pocket, in case it made her mother cross. Sometimes her mother flew into a *tatter*, even if nobody had done anything bad. Everything would be quiet, then the noise would start. Dicky would put his tail between his legs and creep into a corner. He pretended he was asleep, but he wasn't really. He blinked his eyelashes and the hair over his eyes twitched. He was watching because he might have to jump up again in a hurry.

The mother smiled at the teacher when she told her about the hand. "What a terrible girl we have here. What will we do with her?"

When the teacher had gone, the child thought the

mother was in a good humour and tried to talk to her like grown-ups talk, but she got cross *on account of* she'd kept the hand a secret, and people would think she was a bad mother.

She didn't cry either when Mr Lawlor's horse nearly bit her finger off. They brought potatoes on Saturday. They were the best potatoes in the country, big and white and fluffy. They were called *Kerry Blues*.

Mr Lawlor always said, "When we get near the town, the horse always walks faster. He trots in from Station Road, then gallops when he gets to the bridge. Even when I stand up and shout 'Whoa! Whoa there! You black divil!' he still won't whoa!"

When the child heard the clattering and banging, she always ran to get sugar.

The horse rattled down the street, with the potatoes jumping up and down and falling out and Mr Lawlor standing up, holding on to his cap with one hand and the reins with the other. The child waited at the door, her hand stretched flat. When the horse clattered to a halt, Mr Lawlor always fell over.

"*Bad cess* to the two of you."

She giggled as she felt the rubbery lips. The big yellow teeth crunched and the horse's whiskers tickled her palm.

One day his mane got caught in his blinkers. She forgot to keep her right hand flat as she reached up with her left to push the hair out of his eyes. The horse caught her small finger between his teeth. He didn't mean to. It was a mistake. She tried to pull it away, but the teeth bit harder and harder.

Mr Lawlor and her mother were talking grown-ups' talk.

"It was a disgrace," her mother said. "An absolute disgrace."

The child tried to pull her finger out but the horse bit harder. She felt tears rise up behind her eyes. She forced them back again. Still she didn't make a sound. After ages and ages, Mr Lawlor turned to take the reins and the horse let go. She pulled her hand away and hid it behind her back.

"What a good girl she is," Mr Lawlor said.

"In you come, Miss," her mother said in her visitors' voice. "Little girls should be seen and not heard."

"You're a caution," Mr Lawlor said. "A divil entirely."

And he took the reins and trundled away.

iii

Tinker, tailor, soldier, sailor,
Rich man, poor man, beggarman, thief,
Doctor, lawyer...

The small girl hopped along the pavement. She was careful not to step on the lines. The boys stopped playing ball as she got close.

"You're going to be killed."

She stumbled over "Indian chief."

"What did I do?"

"I don't know, but just wait till you get home. You're going to be killed."

Heads down, they looked sideways to see how she was

taking it. They pressed their lips together like the priest did, on the day that the big boys who served Mass drank the Communion wine and couldn't stand up.

She smiled to show she wasn't afraid. She began to walk towards the house. She took tiny steps that got slower and slower. She tried to remember what she had done. She never knew what would make her mother cross. It was never what she thought it was going to be.

Dicky stood outside the door, ears down, tail between his legs. He didn't jump up to say "hello." She scratched him behind the ears.

"What is it, Dicky? What did I do?"

He didn't look up. He lay down and put his head on her shoes. His nose pressed against her white ankle-sock. She got down on her hunkers.

"What is it, Dicks?"

He licked the inside of her wrist. She scratched his nose, and blew gently so that the hair over his eyes parted. He sneezed and rubbed his eyes with the back of his paws.

"It's all right. It'll be all right."

She scratched the place on his back that made his skin scrunch up into a bunch, whispering softly all the time.

"Don't worry, Dickson, I'll mind you. I'll look after you."

After a while, she slid her shoes out from under the little dog, and stood up. She took a deep breath, and knocked on the door. Her heart jumped as her mother pulled it open suddenly, her eyes all sparkly. The red spots stood out on her cheeks.

The child went in. She slid along the wall in the hallway, keeping as far away as possible. She slipped the schoolbag off her shoulder, trailed it along the floor and dropped it in a corner.

"Mammy, I got first in my class."

"Don't you dare speak to me."

"I got first in my music exam, too."

"I'll give you music. After all I've done, this is the thanks I get."

Heart hammering, the child made herself as small as possible. She was afraid to ask what she'd done. She held her breath, and squeezed her eyes tight to try to make herself disappear.

"Look at me while I'm talking to you."

The noise went on and on. She must have done something very bad. She never meant to do anything wrong. She spent her time trying to make things right, like helping the snails who were climbing the wall in the garden. She used to get a stool, pick them up, and reach as high as she could to save them the journey, although they didn't stick very often. They nearly always fell off. And she picked up the snails that came out on the footpath after it rained so that no one stepped on them. And she looked after the spiders. And she minded her daddy, because sometimes he was very pale and quiet.

But there was always something she'd forgotten about.

CHAPTER ELEVEN

Late one evening, I stood outside the small house for the third time. Nobody knew where I was. Everyone thought I was somewhere else. Only the black dog knew. He waited at the top of the lane, Thurber-style, and poked his head around the corner.

"You're going to be killed."

I forced myself to swallow two sleeping pills, retched as the dry particles separated in my mouth. I took the key out of my pocket. Very quietly I put it in the lock and turned it. I held my breath as I pushed the door open.

Nothing had been touched. George Bernard Shaw stared at me and at the chair that lay on its side, the dried and twisted fern, the ashes piled in the fireplace. I dropped my eyes after one quick glance, and stepped inside.

I slid the travel bag off my shoulder and deposited it in a corner. The door banged shut behind me. I spun around to yank it open, but the room tilted and I hit my head on the stairs as I fell.

It was dark when I opened my eyes. At first I couldn't remember where I was. As the shapes began to emerge from the blackness, reality catapulted me into action.

I clawed at my pockets, searching for the sleeping pills. Panic shot through me when I could not find them, then relief as my fingers closed around the bottle.

My whole body shook so much I dropped them. As the white pills scattered, they drew my attention to the threatening shapes, the upturned chair and the triangular frame that contained the throbbing bottomless pit beneath the stairs, the valley of the shadow of death, where all hope had been abandoned.

I hurtled back through the intervening years and reached for the battered teddy-bear, stored in some dark forgotten cupboard.

I had to pretend, to protect.

I had to make things right.

Terrified of unexplained, illogical anger, but programmed to face it, I did what I knew best.

I found the pills and forced them down, then held my breath and ran up the stairs with the energy that sheer terror generates. I lay down on the unmade bed, eyes shut tight, fingers in my ears, panting, a terrified animal immobilised in the steel jaws of a custom-made trap.

CHAPTER TWELVE

The girl sat at the piano, long thin legs twisted around the piano stool.

"Pipe cleaners," her mother said. "Will you look at the cut of her? Telegraph poles. Olive Oyl."

She had a sure touch with nicknames. She crossed her own short legs to display the silk-clad curve of the calf, the slender ankle, the high instep.

"Can you believe she takes size five already? I take size three. I don't know where we got her. It must have been that blow on the head she got as a child, that time she fell off the table. She's never been the same since."

The visitors laughed. They knew that this was the prelude to the story of the tall yellow man, who had called down to her from his high bicycle, "You've the best pair of legs in the country. Better than Betty Grable."

Although no smiles ever coaxed the shy man to repeat the compliment in the presence of witnesses, everyone knew it was a serious matter, since he was a Protestant.

From that day on, the subject of legs was trotted out

regularly. It was accompanied by bright flashes of wit and a becoming modesty, or even a complete forgetfulness of the event, until everyone started to forget. Then, quite suddenly, it came to mind again, was reiterated and heavily underlined.

The girl untwisted her legs. She hunched her shoulders and curled her toes inside the shoes that were far too tight.

She began to play the *Moonlight Sonata*. She liked the first movement best, because it was slow and sad.

The voices and the clink of tea-cups faded, but she could still hear her mother's infectious laughter. It rang louder and longer than anyone else's.

Her father paused in the doorway. She could feel his wide smile. He said "Hello." He never joined in the fun. He went away, belittled in his bewildered gentleness.

"You've such a talented daughter, Ellen."

They didn't mean it. They said it to please.

"Ah well, we all love the music," she replied modestly.

Her faraway look, the smile tinged with sadness, left no doubt about the source of this so-called talent.

Obviously, the legs had taken another route.

When the visitors left, the mother flung open the windows to let the cigarette smoke out. Her movements were swift, like her anger, violent outbursts that operated on a hair-trigger.

The girl took refuge in the third movement.

"Stiff as a poker. Sit up straight. Clumsy lump."

Don't stop. Pretend it's a difficult passage.

"And for Heaven's sake, try to move with the music."

She liked gypsy violins, men with centre partings and gold teeth who swayed and swooped with violins held high, eyes closed.

Feel her push now, forcing her to sway. Fingers faltered. Silver cup jiggled on top of the piano beside the framed photograph from the newspaper. She had cried when she saw it. Rabbit teeth stuck out, pushed out of place from sucking her thumb.

She couldn't bear to see her name in print either. Travelling from place to place, playing at examinations and competitions, palms damp, fingers slippery, heart thumping, trying to smile, trying to please, but nothing was enough, nothing was ever enough. Everyone laughing at her legs, too tall, blush if anyone spoke to her. Only the music was real...it had been her escape, now it was a trap—a trap she herself had laid.

Clytie looked down and to the side, to catch a glimpse of her own beautiful Beleek china reflection in the polished wood of the piano. Perfect oval face, hair parted in the centre, curled and waved into a garland at the nape, trailed over shoulders of unglazed porcelain. The dress was made of iridescent, pearlised ivory, fastened on the right side with four tiny buttons, the other arm bare, where it had slipped down.

Through two world wars, she smiled her sweet smile beside the harnessed waters of the River Erne. Then her luck ran out. She was posted into a battle zone. Third time unlucky for Clytie.

But she was a traitor too. Behind the gentle, smiling

face, she seethed with jealousy. She had her sister buried alive because Helios loved her.

"And try to smile, for Heaven's sake."

But the girl knew too much about smiling...

Hear the door bang. Now it was time for The Silence. Electrically charged silence, it crashed and pounded in waves through the walls. There was never a reason, maybe a letter intercepted, pathetic in its innocence, a story, distorted in the retelling, some imagined injury, an innocent remark turned into a stinging insult.

Escape. She had to escape. Build a fortress of music. Lay a foundation of major and minor scales, cover them with chords. Construct a framework of dominant and diminished chords, reinforce with arpeggios and inversions. Weave the roof with contrary motion, major, minor, harmonic and melodic. Run up the chromatic scale to the small window. Climb in. Bang it shut. Post a sentry. She was safe at last. Nothing could reach her now.

There was only music.

CHAPTER THIRTEEN

I don't remember when I first realised you were here. I wasn't surprised. I forced my eyes open. I glanced around, nervous as a gazelle on the open plains who knows that, out of sight in the long grass, a giant cat watches.

No sound interrupted the silence.

But this was no ordinary silence. No veteran from the wars of childhood could ignore or mistake the vibration. It surged from some dark place, screamed for attention, pounded on the walls. It stormed around the bedroom, creating an atmosphere of terror. It was the same electrically charged silence my mother had perfected all those years ago.

I closed my eyes again, terrified to look at the spot from where the vibration sprang, in case your frail shadow would confirm the inevitable.

Then one day, some day, the second or third day, I got out of bed and walked past you. Without opening my eyes, I felt my way along the wall until I reached the stairs. I fixed my gaze on each foot as I stepped knee-deep into the shadows.

One, two, three, four, five, six, seven,
All good children go to Heaven.

At the bottom, I turned right across the sitting room, to the kitchen.

When they die, their sins are forgiven.
One, two, three, four, five, six, seven.

Then I raised my eyes. What a mess. What a bloody mess.

A slanting tower of dirty dishes leaned precariously in the sink. There were blackened saucepans on the cooker, a layer of encrusted tar covered the oven, food was scattered on the floor.

A small caterpillar humped his way across the refrigerator. A yellow line ran down his back. Yellow spots dotted each side. He gathered up, straightened out, gathered up, straightened out, propelled himself forward until he reached the edge. There, he lost his balance and fell softly, curled on his side.

I tore the top off a herbal tea packet and slid the tiny horseshoe on to the cardboard. I opened the window and put him out on the ledge. I watched as he gathered up, straightened out, gathered up, straightened out, until he disappeared from sight.

How could you?

How could you go away and leave such a mess?

You knew you would never come back.

I glanced at the charts you had placed on the kitchen wall. Delicate drawings of foliage and flowers, dandelion, daffodil, primrose and poppy. Lists of promises:

Agrimony—for those who hide their worries
Cherry Plum—to check irrational thoughts
Aspen—to counteract fear

When your eyes scoured the romantic-sounding names, the hyssop, the fitching and the worthle berries, did you find nothing there to push away the dark clouds that engulfed you...did you find nothing there for despair?

Or did you expect to be found in time?

Was the theatrical scene you engineered a more dramatic version of the familiar attention-grabbing, deathbed scene?

Did you want to make everyone suffer because you could not fulfil some impossible dream...Did you need someone to care about you, to help you through the dark night?

Was it a cry for help that went hopelessly wrong?

No, of course not.

Had that been the case, you'd have chosen a less efficient method.

25 April

On my way back from the shop, I met the woman who lives next door.

"When did you get back?"

"Oh, a day or two..."

"Where are you staying?"

"Here, at the house."

Her face was full of terror. She was pale from sleepless nights.

"What happened?"

"I heard voices in the middle of the night, sirens. There were flashing lights, police, an ambulance."

"What did they say?"

"I don't know. I was afraid to go out. I live alone."

"When did you see her last?"

"That day. Sunday. She was getting into her car, as I came home from the church. She waved at me."

"Do you know why she did it?"

"No."

"Did she leave a note?"

"I don't know."

In the pause that followed, the black dog appeared. He bristled in his bad-tempered way when he saw me, small mean eyes fastened on my face. He crossed in front of me, and raised his back leg, a four-legged dancer, performing an arabesque. A stream of yellow liquid sprayed the weeds at my feet. Then, slowly and deliberately, he wiped stiff paws on the ground as he watched me out of the corner of his eye. The steaming pool overflowed. I stepped aside as it ran towards my shoe.

"Just like the boy."

I tore my eyes from the malevolent, retreating figure.

"What boy?"

"It was before your time."

"What do you mean? What happened?"

"He took pills. They found him the first time but he did it again. It was too late then."

"You mean—he did it in my house? Are you saying he killed himself in my house?"

"Yes. Such a nice boy too."

"How old was he?"

"Twenty, maybe twenty-one."

I watched the concertina of her mouth. Eight lines altogether, seven vertical, neatly spaced. One horizontal, slightly crooked, a self-conscious line.

"I didn't know. Nobody told me."

"Ah well, people don't like to talk about these things. And you're not from around here."

Eyes not quite straight. Which one should I look at, left or right?

"Well, I'm here now, so there's nothing to worry about."

Someone was using my voice again. I smiled my cheerful smile, turned the key in the lock, pushed the door open.

Two suicides.

In my house, two young people have died tragically.

In this game of Russian roulette, will I be the third?

17 May

I've been to telephone the coroner. I have to find out why you cut short your charmed life.

I trailed from telephone box to telephone box. None of them worked. At last I found one. I stood in a long queue. When my turn came, I dialled the number. The machine gulped the money down and cut me off. I telephoned the operator. No one answered.

I trudged on through the rain and found another. I lost my money and waited twenty minutes for the operator to answer. She did not believe me, would not put me through.

"Write in for a refund."

"But the stamp costs more than the call."

"I can't help that."

She hung up.

I took a bus to the General Post Office. My hand shook as I dialled the number.

"Coroner's Office."

"Can you help me, please? Can you give me some information about a young woman..." I tried to remember the phrase. "...who died in suspicious circumstances, no, that's not right, in mysterious circumstances...in Church Close?"

Silence.

"In March, it happened in March. Her name was Rosemary. Did she leave a message? Did she say why?"

Silence.

"It was in my house. I live there."

"It's none of your business."

The man's voice hostile, cold as the grave. The telephone crackled in my hand, a life-support machine abruptly disconnected.

22 May

I'm going to clear up this mess.

I'm going to dust, scrub, purify and purge this house. From top to bottom. I will wipe out every trace of your treachery. Every suggestion, every shadow will be erased. Nothing will remain to remind me of you.

I will paint everything white. White doors, white walls, white windows. The chairs will be white. White, white, white. I'm going to coax the house out of its depression, obliterate the memories, give it back its self-respect, fill it with flowers, make it feel loved again, light the fire.

I'll pick up the threads, go on with my life. Reapply for a telephone. Chase them up. Be firm. Telephone my friends, laugh, have fun. Enjoy myself, carefree, happy-go-lucky, like I used to be.

Whatever you did has nothing to do with me. You rejected life. You made your choice. Life's too short. I've had the house blessed. I can do no more.

Hecuba, why should I weep for you?

28 May

Everything is ready to paint. Every nook, every niche scrubbed and cleaned. I put you out of my mind...even when I found the small teddy-bear spreadeagled under the bed where he had tumbled, unheeded. He sprawled on his back, one leg twisted beneath his ear. His tummy was fat, oblong, like a puppy that had eaten too much. The stuffing leaked from the sole of his foot. One black-button eye looked past me, an anxious little bear, abandoned in a grown-up world.

I took the seashell you filled with semi-precious stones, and put it on the window-ledge outside. Its delicate beauty took me by surprise—the crystal sprinkled with stardust, blue lapis lazuli that Marco Polo found for Kublai Khan, amber that flowed from the wounds of tall trees, banded brown and yellow tiger's eye, malachite, to protect from misfortune.

I don't want to know about these things. I don't want to get too close to you. I don't want my imagination to see you find them in a sunny marketplace, caress them with warm fingers, place them gently in your pocket, polish them, then add them to the collection in the seashell that I found in the same kind of sunny place...

I don't want to know about these things. They tell me too much about you, too much I feel drawn to. They strengthen the bond of sympathy between us and that is dangerous. Much too dangerous.

We communicated instantly. I liked you instinctively. Like attracts like. How much were you like me, with your enthusiasm, your spontaneity and your carefree spirit?

I tried to close my mind to you, even when I found the long strands of your dark hair. I plucked them, one by one, off cushions and pillows.

Transfixed, I held one between thumb and forefinger. It sprang out alive, and nestled in my palm. It followed the lifeline, then crossed the bracelets. It quivered as it touched the pulse. It threaded its way delicately in and out among the blue veins until it reached the elbow. There it curled around my arm.

For five years, this rib of hair was part of you. For five long years your most secret thoughts seeped into it, saturated it. It flourished, glossy and strong in the good days. It drooped, lank and listless in the bad times.

19 June

So much paint. There are pots of white paint everywhere, rollers, brushes, a smell of turpentine. My hair, my clothes, my face, are streaked with paint. It's almost finished, only the space under the stairs to do.

Each time, I find more strands of your dark hair, I pick them up, and add them to the bunch.

Lines from a poem trip lightly into my mind.

To dance to flutes, to dance to lutes
Is delicate and rare:
But it is not sweet with nimble feet
To dance upon the air.

I try to push the words away. They persist, light-heartedly jigging around my brain with tiny tapping feet. Stoical, with arm outstretched and eyes half-closed, I daub at the triangle underneath the stairs. The ominous ground bass growls from somewhere deep inside me. Dark threatening chords grow louder and louder.

Determined to finish, I ignore them. I hold my breath until I almost suffocate. I walk around your tall body. I touch the untouchable. I paint the gallows white.

The bouncing rhythm prances into my head again:

We saw the greasy hempen rope
Hooked to the blackened beam,
And heard the prayer the hangman's snare
Strangled into a scream.

I dip the brush into the thick gloss paint and spread it on the chair that stands innocent now, no evidence of treachery in its prim, upright lines. The sonorous ground bass rumbles to a start again. It's overtaken by the skipping rhythm.

They mocked the swollen purple throat
And the stark and staring eye.

The two rhythms deafen me. The blood pounds in my ears. Make it stop. Please, make it stop.

And a spirit may not walk by night
That is with fetters bound, .
And a spirit may but weep that lies
In such unholy ground.

Stop. Please stop.

The trotting rhythm breaks into a canter. Runaway hooves bolt through my brain.

They hanged him as a beast is hanged,
They did not even toll
A requiem that might have brought
Rest to his startled soul,
But hurriedly they took him out

And hid him in a hole.

I clap my hands over my ears. Rush to the door. I stumble over pots of paint. Chairs overturn.

Get out. Out
Out. Out. Out.

CHAPTER FOURTEEN

7 November

I'm back.

How enchanting the house looks. Immaculate. The gleaming wood reflects the yellow and burnished gold of autumn flowers. Mirrors sparkle. George Bernard Shaw looks down, determined to capture my attention. The dancing firelight plays a game of "catch-as-catch-can" with the shadows. How I love this house, my refuge from the world, my haven.

How normal everything is. The refrigerator drones a comforting hum. Sudden gusts of rain beat against the window panes. Smoke from the fire puffs into the room. I am so happy, warm, comfortable. How foolish I was to get carried away by a too vivid imagination. Like summer, you have come and gone. Now you're lost in the mists of autumn.

How pretty the books look in the flickering firelight. Reach up. Touch them. Run my fingers along the leather bindings. Pick one at random. It falls open in my hands, the discoloured pages mottled. Delicate sheets of tissue protect the engraved plates.

There's rosemary, that's for remembrance.
Pray you love, remember.

The innocent words spring out from the gold-tipped page. I bang it shut. It falls open again.

I am thy father's spirit,
Doomed for a certain time to walk the night...

I slam the book shut, replace it, pick another at random, then another and another. Van Gogh, Marilyn Monroe, Virginia Woolf, Tony Hancock.

I watch, mesmerised, as the unseen hand brings to my attention a disparate cross-section, with one common denominator.

Very quietly, inside me, a single minor chord sounds. Aware of the battle of wills, conscious of the macabre game of Snap you are playing, fear spreads through my body. Tiny spiders scurry down my arms and legs. A snake, slimy with menace, slithers down my spine, then squeezes my insides tight. Each nerve in my body uncoils and stretches until it is taut and ready to snap.

Defiantly, I grit my teeth and take refuge in a colourful paperback. I pause for a moment, close my eyes, choose a spot, put my finger on it and open my eyes.

In the woods by the frozen pond...one of the orderlies found her dead...I'm afraid she's hanged herself.

Sylvia Plath's words scream at me from inside the purple and yellow covers.

My flesh crawls. One by one, the hairs on the back of my neck lift. The minor chords inside me, at first muffled, become deafening.

The temperature in the room drops. Sparks fly from the fire as at last, acknowledging defeat, I turn and lift my eyes.

From the space beneath the stairs, you look back at me, silent and cold as the grave.

ii

While I was away I couldn't get you out of my mind. You went around and around in my head, echoing and re-echoing, through blurred days and sleepless nights.

Everything reminded me of you. You lurked on street corners, on hoardings where stocking advertisements showed slender young legs suspended in mid-air. Whenever I glimpsed televisions in shop windows, they played the same scene—the quick movement of a startled horse, the leering faces of a lynching mob, a body left suspended from a tree, head bowed, hands down by its sides.

Night after night, I walked in my sleep, searching, always searching. Driven by the dream, I ransacked the bedroom, opened the door, ran down the stairs and awoke in the street.

One night, I bolted and chained the door, locked myself in and hid the key. That night I found myself crouched on the ledge of a fifth-floor window.

In an altered state of consciousness, with eyes wide open, I surveyed the weird moonlit landscape. I didn't recognise the ordinary everyday view.

Even the radio, my only friend, turned traitor. The late-night serial described in detail a scene in which a boy was found hanging by his scarf, with purple face and protruding tongue.

I cannot rest.

I had to come back.

It's my house.

You're my responsibility.

I have to be here.

CHAPTER FIFTEEN

24 December

It's Christmas. Happy Christmas.
Cold outside. Colder inside.

I saw a blackbird on a branch. He held an orange berry in his yellow beak. In the street, a girl sprayed a boy into a cocoon of luminous green paint. A man touched a girl's arm. Her face glowed above a red upturned collar as she turned to smile at him.

In the supermarket, sugar spilled from the corners of wrinkled packages. A woman held on to a trolley for support as she surveyed shelves ransacked for a siege.

"Mother of Jesus."

Her life flashed before her eyes as her cry of anguish drowned Rudolph the red-nosed reindeer's bouncing song.

"Mother of Jesus. The stuffing is all gone."

My hair has gone too.

"Just a little trim, please. Just the ends."

"Leave it to me."

Antonio of London, Paris and Rome did not look at me. A massaged and manicured woman threw her arms around his neck and kissed him on the cheek. She whispered something in his ear. They laughed.

I closed my eyes and sank into the fumes of ammonia and lacquer, and the distant chat of parties and boyfriends.

When I opened my eyes, my hair had dried into a nest on the floor. I reached down to touch it. It was soft, so very soft. I squeezed it until the nails bit into my palm.

Antonio of London, Paris and Rome skipped around me with a mirror. He showed me the cruel shape from the left, the right, the back. I watched from the end of a dark tunnel. The gaunt face looked back at me, empty eyes sunken in black rings. Watchful now. Too late.

Like a piranha, he had stripped my bones.

This skull that had a tongue in it and could sing once, now whispered only of death.

At the corner of Grafton Street, a drunk swayed on rubber legs. He collapsed untidily at my feet. He slumped, legs straight out, head on his chest, a puppet without a master. I reached down to help him, but he was too heavy for me. I lost my balance and fell beside him. We sat side by side, legs stretched out on the cold pavement.

He gripped my arm tight. Without looking at me, he raised his head and began to sing.

I'll take you home again, Kathleen,
Across the ocean wide and wild.

His voice was soft and perfectly in tune. His whiskey

breath carried the song into my face. His raised, sand-coloured eyebrows pointed to where each note was pitched.

After the first phrase, his body crumpled. His head dropped limp on to his knees. I tried to breathe deep breaths in the long pause. The bitter wind carried flurries of snowflakes to melt on my exposed neck. Then the careless puppeteer jerked on the strings and he came back from some distant place.

To where your heart has ever been,
Since first you were my bonny bride.

His eyes were full of past hurts. Once he had stood proud and straight and he too had had a dream.

The roses all have left your cheeks
I've watched them fade away and die.

A car drove past and drenched us both with slush. Someone pointed and laughed.

I hoped it was no one who recognised me.

On my feet again, I stopped to listen to children singing Christmas carols.

Silent night, holy night,
All is calm, all is bright.

While the conductor greeted a passing friend, the enthusiastic clatter of a collection box encouraged the tempo. It picked up pace. Another couple of shakes and it gathered speed over the jumps. Neck-and-neck they started the run down the hill and galloped into the home stretch. The collection box took the lead. It rattled past the post to win by a nose.

I do try to pray. I slip into still churches from noisy streets. The plaster saints ignore me. Smug beneath their halos, they stare Heavenwards. Their toeless sandals crush snakes and demons into the earth.

Homeless old men come in from the cold. Hunched in corners, their bleached eyes slide sideways in weatherbeaten faces, watchful for a soft touch.

Hands tipped with long fingernails grasp proffered coins. Then they scratch a little, snooze a little, and shuffle into the outside world on shoes held together with string.

One woman walks backwards down a side aisle. She beats her breast and strokes the feet of each indifferent statue as she passes.

Another prostrates herself face downward on the floor, with arms outstretched. In loud dramatic moans she begs for forgiveness now and at the hour of her death.

I watch people bow, genuflect, finger Rosary beads, light candles. I listen to the murmur from the Confessional box.

So, what is all this praying about?

What is it all about?

Death must have surrendered its secrets to you. What tales you could tell if you would speak—of battles lost and won, of kingdoms in the sky. Is there a Heaven to reward, a Hell to punish us?

If the blessing of the house had released you, I could believe in a life after death. But you cling to the earth.

You've become a footfall on a creaking stair, a shiver down the spine on a winter's night, a skipped heartbeat, a spook. Something that goes bump in the night.

If we live and die like plants and flowers, why do you stay doggedly by my side? Why do you sap my strength?

If death is a never-ending sleep, why do you never sleep?

CHAPTER SIXTEEN

"Bless me, Father, for I have sinned. This is my first Confession."

The *Bonsai* bride, dressed in white, hands joined over smocked voile heart, was transfixed by the hair that sprouted from the priest's ear.

"Tell God what sins you've committed, my child."

"Father, I said a sin."

"And what did you say, my child?"

Breakfast after Mass, in the convent, rashers, sausages, black pudding and brown bread, the squeak of nuns' shoes on over-polished linoleum floors.

"And do you know what she said then, Sister?"

"Father, I said 'bugger.'"

She had heard Jim Mahoney say it, blackcurrant jam smeared over his pale face Now his arms were gone, blown into the air when he lit a match and touched the dynamite the roadmenders had left.

She told his sin to the priest because she had no sin of her own. Now she had committed two, a mortal sin for saying it, and a sacrilege for telling a lie in Confession.

She shuddered and hugged her arms close. She joined her hands tight, and pressed the fingers against her mouth to stop her heart from jumping out on to the floor. The loud piston pumped and rocked her body. Her short puff sleeves quivered. The edge of her veil trembled.

"Tell God you're sorry and say three Hail Marys."

It was all downhill after that.

The pressure to produce a sin on demand opened Pandora's box. Burdened as she was with the sacrilegious millstone, each new revelation brought possibilities of damnation and destruction, of fire and brimstone.

Thou shalt. Thou shalt not.

Thou shalt. Thou shalt not.

God became a monster who raged around the Heavens. He terrorised huddles of small angels. She tried to hop through the minefield of rights and wrongs, never knowing which was which.

The nuns didn't help. They wrenched away the silver music of innocence, distorted it, orchestrated it with harsh dissonants and forced it into the mode of dogma and doctrine.

"How many Gods are there?"

"There is but one God."

"How many persons in one God?"

"There are three persons in one God."

"Was Christ God?"

"Christ said He was God. He proved His claim, therefore He was God."

"What will happen on the Last Day?"

"On the Last Day, God will come in power and glory to reward the good and punish the wicked."

Poor Christ. His humourless, self-appointed "brides" dedicated their dry, narrow lives to banishing love and laughter. The more we laughed, the more we were punished, until, giggling helplessly, we no longer knew what we were laughing at, but like Pavlov's dogs, we knew it must be bad.

"Well, Miss, and what are we laughing at?"

"Nothing, Sister."

"So, we're laughing at nothing, are we?"

Tight, pinched mouth disappeared under a moustache, a hen about to lay a small poisoned egg.

"Well, Miss Troublemaker, we all know what happens to people who laugh at nothing, don't we? Answer me."

"I don't know, Sister."

"So we don't know? Miss Smart-Alec doesn't know."

Flick through her arsenal. Search for a suitable insult.

"Well, the laugh will be on the other side of your face on the Day of Judgement, when Our Saviour calls the just to sit on His right side and banishes the sinners, howling, to burn in Hell for all eternity."

The mouth reappeared under the moustache. She almost choked on her own venom.

"So we find that funny, do we? Well, you'll stand here until you tell us what's so funny. Let the rest of us share the joke."

"Sister, Mary McDermott has to wear a corset up to her armpits to make her flat."

"So that's the filth that's in your mind? Our Blessed Lady listens and turns her eyes away in shame. Is it for this Our Lord was crucified?"

Death, judgement, Heaven, Hell.

Only the nuns who taught music made life bearable. They smiled as they slid oranges down a wide sleeve, or rummaged in deep pockets to produce a crumbling biscuit that smelt of mould, with a piece of fluff attached.

For the most part, the "Holy Marys" who paraded their own virtue and piety treated them with contempt, the sensitive controlled by the insensitive, the musical by the tone-deaf.

Where are they now, those pale humourless nuns, with their sickening scent of sanctity and carbolic soap? Do their narrow, blue-veined hands glide effortlessly over celestial harps, as they ripple through the cosmic hits? Do they strain the glory of the Heavens through their small mean hearts, while Hell vomits in an orgy of non-stop muzak?

CHAPTER SEVENTEEN

New Year's Day

I lay in bed, my head buried under the duvet that protects my eyes from sudden and startling night visions. A car stopped outside. Voices shouted "Happy New Year."

The black dog barked. Somebody was trespassing on his beat. I imagined him staring straight ahead, implacable, as he raised his leg against the wheel of the car to lodge a protest.

"Happy New Year."

There will be no Happy New Year for you. You'll never toboggan like a tomboy again, or bully your old car into life on frosty mornings while the fog of your warm breath lingers on the air.

Music poured from the car radio. I strained to hear. I pulled the covers down and raised my head to listen.

The music floated through the open window, music that was full of tears. It collected under the sloping ceiling and slid down the uneven white walls. It settled on the chest of drawers and the white wicker chair. It filled the room with brooding.

Tchaikovsky. I imagined his head bent over a manuscript, quill in hand, the heart-shaped bearded face full of anguish as he communicated the despair that words can never convey. What could have caused such sorrow?

Then I remembered. It was the final movement of his last symphony, the *Pathétique.* Nine days after its first performance he poisoned himself with arsenic.

It was a lament for his own life. I was listening to the soul secrets, the last testimony of someone who was about to kill himself. Prelude to a suicide.

Warm breath blown through wood, warm fingers on strings conveyed a message that was heavy with grief. He had made his decision to die even before the "Court of Honour" had recommended it. He had sinned. He had sinned because he had loved. He had loved the forbidden love, the love that dared not speak its name. His sin outweighed the joy his music would have brought to the world.

There were songs that would never be sung.

The music trailed off in despair. Even the black dog had the grace to remain silent.

5 January

I cannot get the music out of my head. It spins around and around on the turn-table of my brain. The feelings it arouses are dark and scary.

If only I had listened to your music. I might have noticed the pitch darkening in colour, the lingering farewell before the final crescendo of despair. But like an untrained ear, I listened only to the melody.

1 February

Why? Why? Why?

I have to know. I must find out. I need to know every detail. I need to face the facts. If I knew, I could exorcise the guilt, the horror, the fear.

And what is it you want to tell me?

I pick up your mayday call, but cannot unscramble the message. To be left alone with my imagination is torture of the worst kind.

5 February

I'm going to see your mother again. It's almost a year, time for wounds to have healed. It will be easy now. I'll be discreet, make an excuse, say I've examined the inventory. That is normal. We never had one. She won't know. I'll ask if you have stored anything away, the things I cannot find.

There was a duvet, I remember it well. It filled the bedroom with sunshine and flowers.

7 February

...Was that your shroud? In the panic of the moment, while the ambulance waited with flashing lights and back doors open, did they place your cold body in the softness of the wild flowers, lay you down among the bluebells and the poppies? Did they cover you with buttercups to conceal your fatal error in the warmth of never-ending summer?

15 February

The young man answered the door, unsmiling. I tried to read what lurked behind his eyes. Was it dislike, hostility… Blame? Was it blame?

I followed him into the kitchen. Your mother stood behind an ironing board.

"I was passing by. Dropped in to say hello."

"How nice to see you again."

I perched on a high stool.

"I hate ironing."

"Me too."

"When did you get back?"

"Oh, a day or two."

"Just on a visit?"

I glanced down to hide my eyes. "Mm." I picked up a shirt, laid it face-downwards, turned the sleeves in from the shoulders, then folded it three times, turned it around and arranged the collar.

"How are you?"

"Fine. Absolutely fine."

Silence.

As she finished each garment, I picked it up, folded it and placed it on a pile.

"Have you been away on holiday?"

"You mean in the summer? No, no, we stayed here. There is always such a lot to do."

She kept her eyes down, concentrating on the task. Covertly, I looked into her pitiful, haggard face.

"And you?"

"Me?...Oh, summer, you mean, oh yes, I stayed in London."

"Where do you live in London?"

"Notting Hill."

"They have a carnival there, don't they? I saw something about it on television."

"Yes. It's very colourful. Three days of music and dancing in the streets."

I had heard it in the distance. Powerful loudspeakers ripped through the morning, "Testing, one, two, three." I had stared at the ceiling through the long nights, listened to ghetto-blasters. Beer cans were kicked along the street. Whistles drilled through my head.

"Those men with the long hair..."

"Rastafarians...followers of Bob Marley and Haile Selassie."

"Is their hair real?"

"I think so. One day I looked down from an upstairs window and noticed a bald spot among the dreadlocks."

The clown had popped his head up again. We both started to laugh. As I looked into her older eyes, I remembered I had done it all before. With you.

How could I ask what lay behind your sunny smile when we both smiled the same smile, hiding a black pit of horror and despair behind our laughter?

A photograph I had seen flashed through my mind. A famine victim, shrunken and wizened, held on to a chair for support and smiled for the camera.

But I've become alert now. I have learnt to listen. From my perch on the high stool, I picked up another shirt. Now my ear was tuned to the counter melody, a pavane, a slow dance of death, for a child who has gone away, never to return.

I have come away with a tea-chest that bears your name. Glancing inside, I see it contains a rusty toaster, three teapots and a frying-pan.

16 February

I am haunted by the expression on the young man's face, and the dull emptiness in your mother's eyes.

CHAPTER EIGHTEEN

9 March

Your anniversary.

One whole year and you're still here.

10 March

I had to get away. I had to escape from your powerful presence. Your disapproving eyes burrowed into me as I picked up the keys, pulled on my coat and banged the door shut behind me.

Head down, I walked quickly through dark, wet streets. Each stride took me further away from you. At last, I pushed through swing doors. A kaleidoscope of colour and sound dazzled me.

In the crowded bar, drums and double bass laid down a strong rhythmic foundation. Piano and guitar constructed a framework of melody. They continued to build and build, chorus on chorus. They improvised a mighty tower of music.

I closed my eyes and felt the vibration along my body. Warm honey massaged my head and the tired muscles in my back. It rushed down arms and legs until it reached fingertips and toes. It relaxed the solar plexus and the knotted belly. It lapped around the dark place that held the wounds, the fears and the held-back tears.

At the climax, the instruments intertwined and interlocked. They enclosed me in a sanctuary of music.

Dribbles of notes decorated the impenetrable structure. I felt safe at last. Nothing could touch me. There was only music.

"Would you like a drink?"

In the buzz of the interval, I opened my eyes. I looked up at a young man, dressed in jeans and a checked shirt.

"Can I get you a drink?"

I watched as he sat down beside me. Over a dark stubble, his half-closed right eye bulged, blackened and bruised.

"Have you been fighting?"

He shook his head.

The musicians returned to the stand. They tuned up and threw jokey snatches of tunes from one to another. They put a five-beat bar into a four-beat phrase, slobbered over a syrupy country and western song. They slammed into concrete music, alternating heavy clusters of discords with sudden rhythms tapped on the wood of their instruments.

Several people laughed out loud.

"What happened to you?"

"I tried to hang myself."

I searched the good eye for a glimmer of humour. The

piano player struck a minor chord. He underpinned a soaring introduction with five strong chords. The crowd hushed. A blonde girl began to sing.

Southern trees bear a strange fruit
Blood on the leaves and blood at the root.

"It's a joke, isn't it?"

The man shrugged and turned to look at the musicians. A streak of smoke rose from the top of the guitar where the guitarist had tucked a lighted cigarette.

"Pastoral scene, bulging eye, twisted mouth,

Rain...

Wind...

Sun...

Trees...

Crows...

Here is a strange and bitter crop."

The crowd cheered. The girl smiled and bowed.

"What went wrong?"

"The rope stretched. I fell and hit my eye against the mantelpiece."

"Where? Where did you do it?"

"In a friend's house."

The crowd applauded and called for an encore.

"Hardly good manners."

"What do you mean?"

"Doing it in a friend's house. You could have frightened him to death."

"Oh, I never thought of that."

"Couldn't you have found a more appropriate venue?

Isn't there a book of etiquette, some suicide manual you could have consulted?"

"I doubt it. When the chips are down, it wouldn't be too high on a list of priorities."

"You might at least have done it beautifully."

He looked at me strangely.

"You know, with vine leaves in your hair."

"What on earth are you talking about?"

"Maybe your friend hates illness and death, loathes anything ugly."

"You're weird, you're really weird."

"Not me. Hedda Gabler."

"Ah, I knew I'd heard it before."

The blonde girl started to sing again. The crowd hushed.

"So have I."

He walked home with me. It was late. He had spent his money on drinks. I gave him a cup of coffee and handed him a blanket. He slept on the flowered sofa with his head underneath the stairs, a failed suicide drawn like a moth to a flame.

As he slept, I listened to his night mumblings and tried to guess his dreams.

11 March

You've succeeded.

You laid siege, stormed the fortress of music, my one secret place, my refuge since childhood, where no one else has been.

Nothing is safe from you.
Nothing is sacred.

27 April

Late this afternoon, I walked from Glenageary to the Martello Tower. I looked down into the sea. Waves of suicide pilots bombed the bay. The sun set on their white headbands as wave after wave rose high on the crest of some powerful emotion. They dashed themselves against the huge rocks in a frenzy of self-immolation.

Needles of spray stung my face. The wind pummelled my lungs. I fought to catch my breath. I shouted into the darkening sky, "Help me. Will somebody help me, please."

But the breeze wrenched the words away.

I turned to walk down the hill.

As I passed a row of cottages, a scene captured my attention. In the glow of firelight, I glimpsed a figure in a room. A silhouette sculpted by a master. Thinker with Cello. He sat quite still, absorbed, head bent towards the fingerboard. The scroll and pegs rose above his shoulder.

He straightened up. He became a bird of prey poised to swoop. He attacked with powerful sweeping movements of the bow. Over a long pedal note, he launched arpeggio figures into the darkening sky.

Like a golden eagle with slow graceful sweeps of its outstretched wings, the music of Bach soared in wide circles. Mesmerised as a rabbit who knows it has been marked as prey, I stood still and closed my eyes. I wanted to merge with the fluid phrases, to lose myself forever in the sound.

Powerful yellow claws on feathered legs picked me up. They dipped and wheeled, then soared higher and higher, until I almost reached what I yearned for.

Abruptly, the music stopped. It dropped me to the ground in mid-phrase. The ferry trumpeted its strident departure.

Rivers of tears poured down my face, as if something had activated a scalding fountain inside me. I felt a sharp ache for something I had lost and only the music knew where I could find it.

It had touched the spot where your silence resonates, the lonely prison of my recurring dream.

CHAPTER NINETEEN

2 August, London

Dear Madam

Some time ago we sent you our account showing the service charges due. However, we have not received payment of these charges. If you do not pay within seven days of receiving this notice, then, regrettably, we will have no option but to instruct our solicitors…

27 August, London

Dear Madam

Examination of our records shows that you have no facility for an overdraft with us…

7 November, London

Dear Madam

Judgement has been entered against you in respect of

arrears of service charges. Please make immediate payment in the sum specified in the Writ, plus interest pursuant of Section 35a of the Supreme Court Act, 1981, of 15% per annum, plus an additional payment in respect of solicitors' costs.

15 November

I sold the car.

The beloved Frog has gone to keep the creditors at bay. A man came and took it away. His shoes were wet. Dead leaves clung to the soles.

I sold its secrets too—how to start it on cold mornings, and the twist of the wrist to slip it into reverse. I showed him how to release the windscreen wiper when it sticks.

I listened to the crunch of slow tyres as he trundled away in first gear.

Judas, the Betrayer, I watched until my trusty friend became a tiny dot in the distance.

CHAPTER TWENTY

10 March

I caught sight of myself in a shop window today. At first, I didn't recognise the drab woman who stared back at me. I looked into the dull eyes of the stranger, then realised that behind those eyes my caged thoughts prowled. The weight that bowed her shoulders was you.

Mismatched clothes hung from the skeleton. One glancing blow from you tumbled me from a world of smart haircuts and designer clothes, from long lunches and carefree laughter.

I could never resist a joke. Now I'm left with a bizarre collection of garments and colours. I lack the interest or the energy to coordinate them. They look ridiculous on my haunted frame.

What is the point of all this suffering?

12 March

How I long for someone to care about me.

I never expected betrayal. Friends disappeared when I needed them most. Filled with their own fears and insecurities, they couldn't cope.

The friends I have left are sensitive. I see concern in their eyes, but no one dares to probe. They dread what they may uncover. We conceal our thoughts behind jokes and laughter. While we laugh, a fire rages through my mind. It devours everything in its path.

Acquaintances are embarrassed by my gaunt hollow-eyed appearance, a death-knell at any gathering. Suffering and grief are unacceptable in a winners' world.

The superstitious don't like to stand close to misfortune. It may be contagious.

Even the weak can now be strong at my expense. They pretend concern in bossy voices.

"You're far too thin. We must feed you up."

"Do grow your hair. It doesn't suit you, it's too short. I hope you don't mind, but only a real friend would tell you."

The practical believe I live here to stop the property from devaluing.

"So clever of you to live there..."

The manipulative spring from nowhere. They use the stepping-stones of tragedy and disaster to gain an advantage.

"You're so brave to stay in that house alone. I would be too frightened if someone wasn't there to take care of me."

Immediately, a male arm reaches out in the direction of the helpless baby voice. She turns with a flutter of eyelashes and smiles directly at him. Then she drops her eyes.

In the street, women become silent when I appear.

"Nice day, now."

"Wet today."

"Cold, isn't it?"

When I pass, they cluster together to exercise tranquillised minds. They've all been to the doctor with their "nerves."

When everyone returns to safe, warm homes, I come home to you.

If only I could scream for help. People who create a fuss always get attention. While everyone rushes to make the noise stop, the quiet ones slip away unnoticed...

I've never learnt to scream.

Each night, I keep my appointment with you. Each night, you wait for me to turn the key. You usher me, trembling, into your lonely tomb. I drag myself to the chair by the fireplace. I crouch there and peer fearfully over my shoulder, compelled to search for the one thing I do not want to see.

I never remember if I've eaten...

If only I could sleep, I could get strong. I go to bed at midnight. Five minutes later, I jump up and dress, thinking it's morning. I return to bed and the recurring nightmare catapults me into action. I ransack the house. I run into the street, searching, always searching, desperate to find the thing I have lost.

In ancient times, the Egyptians believed that dreams were messages from the gods. The Greeks believed they were warnings, inspirations and prophecies that came from Zeus, the father of the gods, via Hypnos, the god of sleep, Morpheus, the god of dreams, and Hermes, the winged messenger.

In biblical times, God spoke "the dark speech of the spirit" when deep sleep fell upon men.

But in school, the Catechism said it is forbidden to believe in dreams. Like ghosts and spirits, they have no place in the civilised world.

Yet, night after night, you stand by my bed, your gaze fastened on the curve of my spine. Silence reverberates around the house. It grips me by the throat, powerful, demanding, destructive. I feel the urgency of your need, but I cannot decipher the message behind your silence.

I know all the night sounds: the sudden drunken ramblings of the alcoholic berating his fat wife and his pale frightened child; the black dog who barks into the darkness to keep his own fears at bay; and the chorus of dogs in the distance who pick up his terror and bark in sympathy—two counter tenors, one tenor, two baritones. I hear the sound of police cars and ambulance, and the unsteady steps and mumbled wisdom of a reveller, homeward bound.

I crouch, ready to spring at the slightest change in vibration. The light is switched on to challenge any moving shadow. The door is unlatched. I'm more afraid of you than of the random violence of a sleeping city.

At three o'clock, I am alert. That is the time I fear most. I burrow down underneath the blankets, convinced that a shadow, grotesque and contorted, will appear underneath the stairs. I stop breathing to listen.

What is it you want from me?

What have you left undone?

I search for clues. I go over telephone conversations, try to remember your exact words. We played a game together, you and I. We chatted and laughed, lighthearted, as we probed the mysteries of plumbers and electricians.

Now that death has wrenched away the masks we wore, the face you show is not a face I know. The superficial people we have been to one another have gone. There is nothing here that can be referred to carpenter or plumber, nor can the moments of uncertainty be dissolved in laughter.

We confront one another stripped to the bone.

There are no jokes now.

At dawn, the light peers through the window to stipple the white walls. A door bangs as a man leaves the warmth of his girlfriend's side, to struggle with choke and accelerator.

Later, the children on their way to school dare one another to bang on my door, brave for a moment in a laughing group.

"That's the haunted house."

"A witch lives there."

Almost with relief, I hear the light step of the postman, with his increasing burden of demands forwarded for my immediate attention...

Dear Madam

It has been brought to our attention...

Dear Madam
We refer to our letter...

Dear Madam
As a matter of extreme urgency...

Dear Madam...

Dear Madam...

Dear Madam...

You placed yourself beyond the world of overdrafts and service charges, of managing agents and writs. While you play dead, no postman disturbs your rest, no one demands anything of you, not even the rent.

CHAPTER TWENTY-ONE

The kitchen was empty. Stella slept in her cot and Dicky lay with his head between his paws. The clock chimed once.

The small child climbed on to a chair and pulled herself up on the table. "Look, Dicky. Watch me."

The dog raised his head. Brown eyes looked through the fringe. His nose twitched.

"One, two, three."

She jumped. The red-buttoned shoes landed on the red tiles.

She clambered up again, counted and jumped. The third time, she stumbled and fell head-first.

When she woke up, she was lying on the sofa beside the fire. She felt sick. People looked down at her and whispered to each other.

Uncle David came to the door.

"She's pretending," he said. He put a shining sixpence on the floor. "It's for you."

The child wanted to please. She reached out towards

the silver hound, but the sickness flooded into her mouth.

"Concussion," somebody said.

"I hope it won't come against her later," her mother said.

"She's never been the same since the fall."

"Never been the same."

"She's not right in the head."

"She's daft."

"She's mad."

"She's mad in the head."

25 March

Am I mad? Are you a creation of my over-active imagination, a melody whispered only in my ear?

But I know you're here. I sense you as an animal would, with a sense beyond sight, hearing, touch, smell, taste. We communicate in a language of fine vibrations. We vibrate at the same frequency.

If we were music, I would understand. If we were violins placed side by side, a string plucked, a bow drawn across one, would cause the other to vibrate in sympathy.

Driver and resonator. In the throbbing silence, a string plucked in the depths of my soul is answered by your shimmering silvery presence.

But we are not violins.

Perhaps the string of sympathy that binds us together is not a pure tone. Instead, it vibrates with hidden harmonics, I the fundamental, you a secondary vibration.

But no...

There is no music now.

7 June, London

Dear Madam

We hereby give you notice in accordance with Schedule 19 of the 1980 Housing Act for our proposals to carry out the redecoration and repair of the exterior of the above property.

We attach herewith copies of the tenders which have been obtained and confirm that the works will comprise the complete repairs and redecoration of the whole of the external parts of the building. This will include the front drive area, the roof covering, the cold-water tanks and associated pipework and all dangerous and structurally defective brickwork.

As you will appreciate, under the terms of our management agreement, we are unable to instruct contractors to proceed with the work for which no monies are available, and owing to the large amount involved, we have decided to demand these monies in two phases.

You will note from the attached schedule that the two right-hand columns indicate the 60 per cent that we require now and a further 40 per cent that will be required in two months' time. We would confirm that we will forward a separate demand for the latter amount of money and include therein any adjustments that are due to be made.

1 July

"Get down on the floor. *Down*, I said, *down*."

A voice barked the command. All activity ceased. I turned to look at a man dressed in sweater, jeans and runners. He stood inside the door of the shop, a block of wood in his raised hand.

"Down."

He padded among us, wrenched watches from wrists, rings from fingers. Dilated pupils stared down at me.

"Don't move."

He grabbed my handbag, yanked it open, stuffed the notes into his pocket, tossed the bag on to the floor, walked out, slammed the door and disappeared with the money I had borrowed from friends to pay the overdue bills.

I glanced around. Everyone lay face down. I alone lay on my back, out of touch with the new customs.

12 August, London

Dear Madam

For us to carry out the proposed redecoration, it is necessary for all repairs to the frames, glass, etc. to be carried out first. We are, therefore, writing to give notice that we will carry out these repairs on your behalf whilst the major repairs are being carried out, and that each leaseholder will meet their individual costs accordingly. These will be demanded by ourselves from you as a separate charge, based on the amount of work that was carried out to your individual windows.

We would add that if any further delays occur in the payment of the 60 per cent already demanded, this will result in a possibility of an increase in the contract figure.

We look forward to receiving your cheque by return.

16 September, London

Dear Madam

The service charge demanded for the second half of the year has not been received by us.

We would draw your attention to the fact that failure by leaseholders to pay these charges is unlawful and constitutes grounds for repossession.

This is the final application for payment within seven days. If this notice is ignored, proceedings will be taken in Court without further warning.

ii

The rhythm of my body has become confused. Day after day, night after night, my life drains away on a river of red.

I go through the motions of living on a treadmill of debt, demands and threats, while you sit on top of my brain and demand my attention. In the darkness of the night, your tormented thoughts beckon to me.

If only I could cry.

Instead, a stream of guilt, terror and despair rushes through me.

I never learnt to cry.
I bleed when I should cry.

I wonder if spring will ever come again...
If I'll ever laugh again...
I wonder if I'll ever be myself again.

25 September

As I came from the shop, a man called out, "Come and have a cup of coffee."

I walked through the open green door and sat in an armchair by the fire. The black dog poked his head around the door. Just checking.

"Monsieur Poirot!"

We both laughed. I took the cup of coffee he offered.

He looked directly at me. "I was there, you know."

I looked at his face, puzzled. "Where?"

"That night...in your house. I was there."

The knot in my stomach tightened. I sensed danger, and shook my head to stop him. He didn't notice.

"I heard a noise in the middle of the night, and got out of bed to look through the window. There were people outside your house."

I opened my mouth to stop him. I couldn't push the words out of my throat.

"I pulled my coat over my pyjamas, and went to see what was happening."

I tried to stand up to leave. My body refused to obey the command.

As he stumbled over the words, his eyes bulged with

terror. They looked without seeing. A nervous tic flickered at the corner of his right eye. He went on talking and talking.

When he'd reached the house he had found the door open. A lamp projected the shadow of a figure on to the wall.

In panic he had knocked the lamp over. The shadow moved up the wall and across the ceiling. He turned and saw you under the stairs. He shouted, touched your arm. Your body was cold and stiff.

He stopped speaking for a moment. In the silence he began to rock gently to and fro as if he were sitting on a rocking chair.

"I ran into the kitchen and grabbed the breadknife. I slashed and slashed at the rope that held her. Her body fell on top of me, and knocked me down."

...The breadknife. He cut you down with this breadknife. This breadknife with the bent blade and the three missing teeth.

I eat the bread
Cut by the knife
That slashed at the rope
That held you by the neck
Until you were dead.

I'm leaving. I can go no further living in your darkness, while your giant shadow looms over me.

Without me you might not exist. Together we're a disastrous combination. We feed on one another.

I give you life. In return, you fill me with terror. Like a monstrous cuckoo, you forced your way into the nest. I cling to the edge, helpless as a fledgeling.

I barely knew you. You're not my responsibility. You made a choice. You forfeited your life, discarded it like an out-of-fashion dress. Now you must leave me with mine.

I have agonised too long. I've done nothing wrong.

This time, I'll walk away from you. I'll sell the house and never come back.

CHAPTER TWENTY-TWO

31 December

I'm back.

It all went wrong. Seven agents tried to sell the house. None succeeded. How could they? It has been desecrated by your action. What you did will echo and re-echo through the generations. The horror it cradled in its arms seeps into the walls. The pain it contains can never be erased. Every breath, every sigh, every sob, absorbed forever into its heavy beams.

Each agent added a bill for advertising to the mountain of debt I have accumulated.

I sold everything. I sold the piano. It wasn't enough. I sold my violin. It still wasn't enough. I sold the pictures. It was never enough. I tried to sell the flat. The sale fell through.

I cannot get away from you.

Once, I slipped into a cinema to lose myself in the darkness. The title flashed on the screen. It was *Wetherby*, the secret name I give you in my diary. It told the story of a twenty-five-year-old man who committed suicide in the house of a stranger.

Whatever I do, wherever I am, you're there. If I end up sleeping on a bench, you will find me. You'll stand by my side in the freezing nights, your accusing stare sending shivers down my spine.

7 January

That girl who came to the door just now...

"Is this house for sale?"

"Yes."

"Could I come in and have a look?"

Wide smile, gap between front teeth, a sprinkle of freckles.

"The agent is dealing with it."

I turned to get a card from my handbag.

"Couldn't you let me see it? Please?"

"I'd prefer it if you made an appointment with the agent."

"Please. I can't come back until next week. It may be sold by then."

She came in, enthusiastic, spontaneous, touching wood, books, ornaments.

"It's so pretty. Let me look upstairs. Please."

I could hear quick, light footsteps in the bedroom, then a quick dash downstairs.

"It's like a doll's house."

I felt terror creeping up my spine. She stood directly under the new telephone wire. It coiled like a noose above her head, where the engineers had left it to await my return. She turned to smile at me. I looked into your eyes, at your hair.

Then she turned and walked away.

I am caught in your trap. When I try to free myself, you punish me. The more I struggle, the more entangled I become. Now, you warn me not to sell the house. If I do, it will ensnare another young life.

Never two without three.

CHAPTER TWENTY-THREE

While I was away, I switched the radio on one morning. I heard a woman's voice.

"It's a year since my sister's suicide."

I turned up the sound.

"I feel so guilty. I think of the things I might have done to stop her."

I listened, transfixed.

"The feelings intensify as time goes by, but I don't talk about it. I don't want to upset anyone."

At the end of the programme, the presenter, a psychologist, offered a leaflet to listeners. She summed up: "Even if one wonders if a suicide could have been prevented, there is no need to carry so much unreasonable guilt around."

I tried to write to the BBC for the leaflet. My handwriting sprawled across the page. I was filled with shame when the jagged, unformed letters lunged out of control.

I tore it up.

One day, I stood at the bend in the street where the mighty prow of the BBC sails into Regent Street.

I pushed open the heavy door and walked into the foyer. My eyes flicked over marble walls, a glass case, ostrich-egg lamps, security men. To the right, clock, counter, chrysanthemums. I walked over the blue carpet.

The receptionist looked up with a smile. I smiled back, and asked for the leaflet.

"Let's see..." She glanced at a list. "Just one moment."

She picked up the telephone and asked for the presenter by name. Panic-stricken, I tried to stop her.

"Please don't disturb her. I didn't realise...I thought I could just take one..."

"It's no trouble."

"Really, it's not important. I'm in a hurry. I can't wait. I'll call another time."

"She's on her way down."

Too late. No escape. I was trapped. I turned my back and began to read the roll of honour to the right of the counter.

Alway—Barker—Bates—Betler—Binks—Brown—

I glanced around to judge the distance between me and the door. The girl behind the desk smiled again. "She'll be down in a moment."

Parker—Partridge—Patten—Plowden—Proctor—

The lift whirred. The words blurred.

Wharton—White—Wigzell—Wilkey—Williams—

I turned around. A girl walked towards me, open, smiling.

Sudden tears threatened. Any act of kindness makes

me want to break down.

"For a friend," I muttered. I took the yellow pages from her.

I turned and fled from her soft, alert eyes. I ran from the thing I craved—someone who might understand. I pushed through the door, out into the street. Only the Heavens wept unashamedly.

I joined the lunchtime throng as they bobbed along under umbrellas, a sea of dripping mushrooms. I followed them past the small Nash church and the tall buildings. I turned into the side entrance of Peter Robinson, and searched for a place where I could be alone. I ran down the escalator, and found myself in a corner of the lingerie department among the oyster-satin petticoats and the black nightdresses.

I gripped the sodden yellow leaflet with the orange headlines, and haemorrhaged among the young girls' dreams while a pounding beat bullied a banal lyric.

I called to make an appointment with my doctor, but he had died while I was away. With a grand flourish, he had his ashes scattered over a race-course. One final flutter, an each-way bet.

Someone recommended another doctor. "Take this number. Great friend of mine. She'll take good care of you."

I called the number.

"This is my home," she said coldly. "Please don't call here. Make an appointment with my secretary."

I found another doctor. Incoherent, I blurted, "A

young girl died in my house. I don't know why she did it. She's trying to tell me something. There's something she has to do. I can't pick it up."

He referred me to a psychiatrist. "I walk in my sleep...have nightmares... maybe it was my fault...maybe the house..."

"Grief."

"But I hardly knew her."

"Grief," he repeated. He was a man of few words.

"It's more than that."

"Grief," he said, looking grave and important. He reached for a prescription pad. "Take these. Call me any time."

I swallowed the tongue-swelling mothballs. My silent footsteps trudged knee-deep through the streets and waded unheeding through the fat envelopes that follow me wherever I go.

Drowsy inside a mosquito net, I lazily observed the world outside.

Only you were real. A mosquito trapped inside the net, you buzzed and dive-bombed. You seethed, biting and stinging. You pierced me with sharp needles. You sawed into my brain without mercy.

In the desperate times I called the psychiatrist. He was always busy. His secretary refused to put me through.

"Sorry about that. Getting married soon. Spot of pre-marital tension," he said later.

I went to the clinic. They sent me for tests.

Clinic—hospital—clinic—specialist.

The specialist sat, a strict headmistress, behind a polished desk. Two children, impeccable in school uniforms, framed in silver, smiled out at her, a boy and a girl.

I tried to tell her about you. She showed no interest. She glanced at the letter from the clinic and examined me briefly. "Fibroids. Hysterectomy as soon as possible."

Out in the street, I held on to the railings. Her words pounded in my ears.

If she'd bothered to ask, I could have told her that she could cut you out of my body and you would bend my shoulders: they could open up my back and you would coil around my brain: they could shock you out of my brain and you would curl up in my heart.

I called the psychiatrist. He picked up the telephone himself. His secretary must have succumbed to "post-marital tension."

"Don't give it a thought," he said. "You're an excellent specimen for surgery."

I tried other doctors, but when I looked at their eyes, I knew they wouldn't understand, and left without bothering to speak.

One last try. Another surgery. A doctor dressed in a white coat. Everything tumbled out, jumbled up.

His moustache seemed to be pasted on crooked, a huge propeller on a small aircraft.

I mentioned fibroids. He perked up. The moustache readjusted itself, straight and centred.

"Well then, it's hysterectomy for you, my girl. I'll refer you to a specialist. Hope you're insured. First class all the way."

I hadn't the heart to mention that insurance was a luxury I could no longer afford.

Another appointment. Another examination. Another specialist, a tall grave man who listened to me.

"Let's try a prescription."

"No operation...?"

"No, let's try something else."

I sat up. I looked down at my feet. They protruded from underneath the sheet. I focused on two gold socks with black spots.

"I've never been so happy."

Some days later, I telephoned the doctor with the moustache. I asked his secretary to put the specialist's letter on his desk.

His voice came on the line. "Hysterectomy for you, my girl. Hope you're insured. First class all the way."

"No, no, you've got it wrong..."

"First class all the way."

I hung up, stunned, then dialled the number again. "It's a mistake. I have a prescription. I'm getting better."

"No. No mistake. First class all the way, my girl."

I had been so certain. I went over the scene in my head. I remembered the look on the specialist's face, the surge of relief, the gold socks. I had the pills he prescribed in my pocket.

I went back to see the specialist.

"I'm sorry, he's not here."

"Not here?"

"He's on holiday."

"When will he be back?"

"He's abroad. He won't be back for a couple of months."

"I have to talk to him."

"Can I help you?"

"I don't know. I thought he said I didn't need an operation. I'm sure that's what he said. The doctor says I've got it wrong."

"Let me have your address and I'll write to you as soon as he gets back."

I stayed with a friend that night and tore a lamp from the bedroom wall in my sleep.

"She's never been the same since the fall."

"Never been the same."

"She's not right in the head."

"She's mad. She's mad in the head."

21 January

You've moved closer. No defined edges separate us. I can hardly tell which is you and which is me.

It's as if the worst instant of your life has been singled out. You are frozen in that moment. Condemned to live with the one thing you wanted to escape, the hidden torment petrified into perpetual reality. By some accident of time or place, I am compelled to share that moment with you.

You cling to me and I'm not strong enough to support

your weight.

One mood reverberates between us. It unites us. Your isolation fuses with the savage loneliness that sinks its claws into me, gnaws at me, tears me apart. From a deep pit of desolation, I reach out in sympathy to you. I know you want me with you, but I'm tired. So very tired.

Your unique discord hangs in the air. You depend on me to resolve it. Sometimes a shadow lurks at the edge of my mind. I grasp at it, but it is elusive and fleeting. It slips away before I can catch it by the tail.

You punish me constantly for my stupidity, the dunce in the corner. The ache in my back is an ever-present reminder of your anger.

"What happened to you?" the physiotherapist asked.

"I fell down the stairs. Three times."

"Three times?"

"In one evening."

Owl eyes studied me from under candyfloss hair.

I wanted to tell her that each time I got to the step where the mark stained the pale wood, your invisible hand refused to let me pass. That you pushed.

I remained silent.

"I'll show you some exercises to strengthen your spine."

She lay on the floor. Her lithe body bounced up, down, up, down, on the small of her back. She curled up and tipped her knees and head together ten times.

"Now, when you get up, do it like this."

She rolled on to her side, then on to her knees, and stood up.

"Lie down now. I'll put you in traction. That may help."

I lay down. She snapped leather thongs on my ankles, set a timer and turned the machine on. I felt the weight wrench my body.

"Telephone call, Sue. It's the boyfriend."

She smiled down at me, glowing. "Back in a minute."

Stretched on the rack of your agony, how could I tell her that you hold me prisoner in the dungeon of your despair? While I grow weaker, you grow stronger, puffing yourself up from the leavings of my life.

Sometimes at night now, my body freezes. I cannot move or call out. Catatonic, I present you with the perfect opportunity to storm my shrunken frame.

It would break my heart to think I might never see another spring.

Never see a purple crocus pierce the soil or a primrose unfurl.

Never climb a ladder and peer into a bird's nest to count the eggs.

Or hear the joyful cadenza of a robin or the wild song of the geese.

ii

26 February, London

Dear Madam

We are writing to inform you that the freehold of the block of which you are a leaseholder has been acquired by a Property Development Company.

They have notified us that they intend:

a) to build a penthouse;

b) to turn the drive into a car-parking area.

This, of course, means that the work which has just been completed by us (i.e. the front drive area, the roof covering, the cold-water tanks and associated pipework) will have to be undone.

We have, therefore, decided that, although it will no doubt be a long and expensive process, litigation is our only course of action.

The cost will be shared out among the leaseholders and added to the twice-yearly service charge.

We will be writing to let you know what your initial contribution will be, and will keep you informed what further monies will be required.

Please send a cheque by return *for the work which has already been done, otherwise...*

9 March

When I saw you last, I was a guest in my own house. You sat on the flowered sofa. We had tea and ginger-nut biscuits.

"How are things?"

"Great. Absolutely marvellous."

"And the house?"

"Perfect. I love it...You don't want it back, do you? That's not why you're here?"

"No. Not yet. I just wanted to see everything is all right."

"Everything is wonderful. Couldn't be better."

Two weeks later, you were dead.

I sit on the sofa now. I take up exactly the same space. If I reach out I can touch the stairs with my left hand.

It's long past midnight. There's a strange feeling in the house. It quickens my pulse and kneads my insides like baker's dough. It makes my hair stand on end.

I try repeatedly to muster the strength to propel myself forward, to escape into the darkness beyond the front door, but my body doesn't respond.

The telephone rests silent on a small table underneath the stairs, a lifeline with no one at the other end.

Is this the moment I have feared, the final struggle between us?

I have hidden you, protected you, lived with you for three years. I can go no further. If it's your world of shadow that wins, I surrender. If you want to be the king of the castle, the driver, the fundamental, good luck.

You left me a legacy of terror.

I can leave only a legacy of debt.

There is a deathly hush. I hear no night people, no dogs, no distant sounds. Even the soothing hum of the refrigerator and the ticking of the clock have stopped. This is a different kind of silence, motionless, spine-chilling, an eerie feeling of timelessness, as if the world has stopped breathing.

My head is on fire. Blood pulsates in my eardrums. The dormant, rutted crevices of my brain distend. The slightest movement will detonate the explosives packed inside my head.

There are no boundaries in my mind.

The lurking shadows sweep them away.

The unacceptable irrational feelings, driven underground for so long, make a stand, then storm my last pathetic defences.

In the highly charged atmosphere, the ground bass that lurked in the background swirls and churns, then surges up to swamp me. Logical, rational thoughts are swept away as icy serpents of fear crawl through my body.

Without looking, I know what lies behind my back. A coal-black pit slides open. It stretches back, noiseless, ominous. I have never known such darkness. I'm afraid I will topple in and disappear forever.

Its gaping mouth draws me like a magnet. It yearns towards me, offers me total oblivion deep in the centre of the earth.

I teeter on the edge, struggle to push myself forward. It reaches out to draw me back. I try to resist the strong magnetic pull. My flesh crawls and cold perspiration runs down my face on to my hands.

I am trapped between two hostile worlds. I have nothing to live for and nothing to die for.

I hang suspended between earth and Hell. I belong in neither.

Totally alone in the middle of the night, I gather my strength and struggle to push the words out.

After an eternity, I hear my voice cry, "O God, help me. Please help me."

The words break the spell. They give me energy.

With the final flutter of a dying bird's wing, I propel myself forward and begin to crawl on my hands and knees across the floor, until I reach the stairs.

This staircase once handed out death. This time it bestows life.

Slowly and painfully, I drag the dead weight of my body from step to step until I reach the top.

With a last effort, I pull myself on to the bed. I collapse with exhaustion as the first taper of light touches the sky, and fall into a long, dreamless sleep.

CHAPTER TWENTY-FOUR

After that night, everything began to change. I became aware of the house again. I had been too preoccupied to pay attention to its needs. Now I tuned in to its distress. It cowered, vulnerable as a small frightened child. A victim of victims. With its painful memories tucked away, it had tried to please, but nothing was enough. Nothing had ever been enough.

Through the years it had played its familiar pleasing role. Each song-thrush that came along, all carefree and freckled, became a threat to this small garden snail. The singing stopped. The powerful beak picked up the shell and hammered it against a stone, determined to devour the defenceless creature huddled inside.

So I spring-cleaned it. I bathed its wounds, bound its scars. I listened to its story. Then I painted it. Pink. The colour of love. I brushed healing balm over every inch of its uneven walls. Loved and appreciated again, it came back to life. Cradled in loving arms, it glowed. It blossomed. It forgave.

Hedging my bets, in case there was a God, I had it blessed again.

In nomine Patris, et Filii, et Spiritui Sancti.

And still I wondered...

You remained. You had not managed to communicate your message but I was no longer afraid of you.

I went to the market and bought armfuls of flowers. I filled every corner with white lilac, daffodils and freesias, with roses and primroses. Then I lit the fire.

It was almost perfect again.

15 March

A small white square fell out of the cupboard where I hide the unopened envelopes. The letter was signed by the tall grave doctor.

This is to confirm that I said you did not need an operation.

17 March

I read in the newspaper today that the doctor who insisted I should "go first class all the way" had died. They said in his obituary that he showed such dedication, he worked right up to the end.

ii

This began a time of coincidence. Images appeared in dreams or in my thoughts. They dissolved and reappeared in concrete form. Three strands woven into one perfect plait.

I watched the timeless, graceful dance, listened to the

canon. "Dovetailing," I called it.

I dreamt of butterflies. Night after night, flashes of coloured wings flew past. They signalled to me. They paused, opening and closing their wings.

As if by magic, a friend sent me two large silk butterflies, one pink, one green and gold. Spotted and striped, the fine material stretched over a wire frame to form racquet-shaped wings, the body divided into segments with silk thread. Their heads were small, the eyes bulbous. Legs and antennae were long and spindly.

I pinned the pink one on the curtain, and the green and gold one underneath the stairs.

One evening I came home, and noticed that a caterpillar had crept under the pink butterfly. Unconcerned and unafraid, it sheltered under this mighty Colossus, this surrogate mother.

I examined it carefully without disturbing it. It was green and clean-shaven, spotted with black, striped with darker green and white. It was perfectly at ease. I glanced at it from time to time during the evening to make sure I hadn't imagined it.

At bedtime, I came down to say goodnight. It had disappeared. I searched everywhere. I examined the curtain , shook it, checked the window-ledge and the floor. It was nowhere to be found.

Heavy with disappointment, I said aloud, "What song can I sing for a caterpillar who has lost its way?" Automatically I reached over and switched on the radio for comfort. The announcer's voice replied to my question. "We have a special request for you. We will play 'Papillons' by Schumann."

As the piano music started, the caterpillar appeared and came *lolloping* down the curtain at great speed. She gathered up, straightened out, gathered up, straightened out, until she reached the window-ledge.

I christened her Titania. The window became her home. Every morning I left a salad for her, lettuce leaves, nettles, cabbage and buckthorn, garnished with a little clover or shamrock. Lettuce was her favourite food. She munched through each leaf and left it fragile as a lace doily. One day she decided that she had stayed long enough and disappeared again.

This was such a time of change and hope, I felt something was about to happen. I felt like a caterpillar myself, pupating inside a silk cocoon, waiting to emerge, with wings soft and crumpled.

I had gained such confidence, I didn't think twice about locking the door and returning to London.

CHAPTER TWENTY-FIVE

London

One day I took a short-cut from Regent Street to Piccadilly. I walked through the archway into Swallow Street. The turbaned and moustached man outside the Indian restaurant smiled.

Around the corner, the tall windows, green roof, the spire, clock and weather-vane of St James's Church came into view.

My eye ran along the dark blue railings. I turned left into Piccadilly and walked towards the bright lights and the statue of Eros.

A little voice inside me whispered, "You've always wanted to see what that church was like inside."

"Yes, I know," I replied.

"Why not do it now?"

"Another time."

"But you hardly ever come this way."

"Yes, I know."

"So what's wrong with now?"

"Well I'd have to cross the street. I'm almost at

Piccadilly Circus."

"So what's the big deal. It will take five minutes."

"Yes, I know, but..."

"So what have you got to lose?"

I stopped. I crossed over at the lights and made my way back, past the blue railings, in through the gate, and across the courtyard between the magnolia and the Indian bean tree.

The church was beautiful. It gave the impression of being all white and gold. It was a church of pillars and galleries, of carved wood and cherub heads.

It didn't tower over me, dark and gloomy, waiting to whack me over the knuckles if I made a noise. It was a church that didn't mind being disturbed. It knew all about disturbances. A bomb had almost destroyed it during the war.

I examined the carved baptismal font. A serpent coiled around the shaft, the Tree of Life. Adam and Eve stood on each side. I imagined a newborn William Blake surprised by water and salt, as he was cleansed of original sin in the name of the Holy Trinity.

When I turned to leave, I noticed a memorial to Charles Cotton of Beresford Dale, "Friend of Izaak Walton," who had been buried in the church in 1687. It seemed unfair to have had a friend so famous that you could end up playing second fiddle on your own tombstone. A supporting role even in death. Like Greyfriars Bobby. Three hundred years on, with a fame time-span of fifteen minutes, choosing a famous friend for posterity could be a tricky business.

This matter occupied my thoughts as I gathered up a handful of leaflets at the church door, and walked out into the Piccadilly sunshine.

Propped up in bed that night, I leafed through pamphlets on church services at St James's, lunchtime recitals, seminars and workshops.

I read about psychotherapy for the first time.

CHAPTER TWENTY-SIX

21 March

I sat in a room with white walls. It was bare except for two chairs. A psychotherapist sat opposite. His face was pale, almost transparent.

I mentioned you.

"She's been dead for three years but her ghost still haunts the house. I feel her presence there."

I watched him carefully. He didn't seem to be shocked.

"I know she wants to tell me something, but I can't pick it up."

I paused. His face hadn't changed. He didn't seem to think I was mad. Encouraged, but still wary, I continued. "I walk in my sleep too. I have a recurring nightmare. It never changes. I wake up ransacking the house, or in the street, or on the window-ledge, searching for something, always searching. I don't know what I'm searching for. Once I asked a friend to sleep in a camp bed to block the front door. He woke up in the middle of the night and watched as I lifted him and the bed, unbolted the door, undid the locks, and walked out. He said my eyes were open."

"Tell me about the dream."

"The dream? I thought dreams were nonsense. The Catechism says, 'Thou shalt not believe in dreams, incantations or spells.'"

He smiled. His eyes were the colour of soft toffees.

"We can go back into the dream you know. Explore it. Try to find what you're searching for."

"You mean now?"

"Yes. It's called a waking dream."

I thought for a moment. "But supposing––"

I stopped. In my imagination I saw myself rampaging around the bare white room, ripping it apart in the search.

"It's all right. There's nothing to be afraid of."

"OK, let's give it a try."

"Close your eyes."

I closed my eyes.

"What's the dream about?"

"I'm buried alive, deep in the centre of the earth. Nobody knows I'm there. No one will ever find me."

"Why are you there?"

"I've lost something."

"What have you lost?"

"I don't know."

"Can you describe it?"

"No. I only know that it's tiny. It would fit in a corner of my pocket, or in the centre of my palm, in the hollow between the head and the heart lines."

Back in the dream, incarcerated in the tomb, I surveyed

the solid rock walls, examined the floor, the low ceiling. It was empty. There was nothing there, only the dust of ages on the patterned floor, and myself, buried alive.

"What are you looking for?"

"I don't know."

"What have you lost?"

"I can't remember."

"Try. Try to remember."

"I can't."

Impassive, the silent tomb waited.

"Try to remember."

I tried to push through the dark mass that blocked the memory.

"You *do* remember."

Suddenly the world stopped turning. In the stillness, something brushed against the nape of my neck with the delicate caress of an angel's wing. A tiny seed stirred at the base of my skull. Firmly rooted in or near the hypothalamus gland, it breathed its first puff of air. Challenged by this barely perceptive inner vibration, my five senses took a back seat. The sixth sense, primed for this moment, took charge. New life that had lain dormant sprang into action.

In one continuous movement a minuscule plant appeared. Stem and leaves splayed through my head and a sunflower bud plopped out in the centre of my forehead. Each petal unfolded until it burst into bloom to reveal the huge dark eye. It filled the screen of my brow, a surrealist canvas painted with one stroke of a brush.

I heard my own incredulous voice.

"My God. I lost the connection. I lost the spiritual connection." Appalled, I opened my eyes. I peered at the man's head outlined against the light that poured through the window.

"I got cut off..."

I floundered. I searched for the words. There are never words to say the really important things.

"You know...from knowing that there's life after death."

Blood rushed into my face.

"That's what she was trying to tell me. That was it."

I struggled to catch my breath.

The man's voice sounded again.

"Come out of the tomb now."

"I can't."

Still in the dream, I searched for an opening, some way to get out.

"I can't get out. There are no doors or windows."

"What's outside?"

"Huge mountains. Nothing growing very much."

As soon as I began to describe the scene, the sunflower stirred. Long fingers stretched. They reached outside and beyond me. They sent golden rays in all directions. The gigantic eye continued to expand, while I remained a microscopic stigma fed on its pollen. It swept every obstacle aside. No prison could hold, no tomb could contain, nothing could stop the thrust of the mighty flowering plant as it yearned towards the light.

It came to rest only when it arrived at its destination. Dark eye and yellow petals of the sunflower mirrored golden eye and golden rays of the sun. I basked in the brilliant light.

"Where are you now?"

"On top of a mountain. There's a huge abyss and a mountain on the other side."

"What else can you see?"

I paused for a long time.

"I see the figure of Christ on the other mountain."

"Can you see the expression on his face?"

"No. The light's too strong. But he's dressed in a red robe."

Mesmerised, I watched the vivid picture. The tall figure faced me across the ravine. One leap was all that separated us.

Far, far away, I heard a voice.

"Breathe." I felt a hand on my shoulder. I ignored it.

"Breathe." The voice sounded urgent. I made an attempt to respond, but however hard I tried, I couldn't kickstart my lungs.

"Breathe."

I struggled. I fought to catch my breath. At last I sucked in some air. It encountered a blockage. Another gulp and a floodgate opened. Again the blood rushed into my face. I heard my own quick shallow breathing. A deluge of long-forgotten feelings rushed through.

I opened my eyes and looked at the man who stood beside me.

A waterfall of tears poured down my face. Not the sniffly sorry-for-myself tears, but huge splashes that soaked the front of my sweater. I tried to speak. No words came. He handed me a box of tissues, took the few paces back to his chair and sat down. I leaned forward and struggled to push the words out. At last I managed to say, "How could I have been so stupid?"

Toffee eyes regarded me steadily.

"She got stuck. I couldn't help her. I didn't know that there was anywhere for her to go. I was lost myself. I had given up. All that stuff in school about hell, all that ranting and raving from pulpits, all those nuns..."

A car alarm pierced the air, then died down.

"I couldn't handle it. I just gave up. But it's not like that at all."

I stumbled over the words, struggled to make sense. An image popped into my head. The small child sat in a meadow that was filled with buttercups and cowslips. A necklace of daisies hung around her neck. Bracelets encircled the small wrists. The little dog snuggled up beside her. Garlands of daisies dangled from his ears. They coiled around his neck. They hung from his tail.

She picked the small flowers one by one from a bunch on her lap. She slit each stem with her thumbnail, and threaded another through.

She joined the first and the last, and held up the circle of white and gold to admire it. She placed it around the furry white head of the dog, like a halo.

Then she became very serious. She smoothed down the bright red dress that had a spider embroidered on the front. She screwed up her face for a moment while she thought. Then she turned around, put her arms around the dog, parted his fringe, put her forehead against his, and looked straight into his eyes.

"You see Dicks, Nip Heneghan got run over *on account of* he ran out on the street without looking. That's why you have to be very very careful. The man in the lorry didn't see him. It was a mistake. He didn't mean to run over him. But when dogs die, we have to close our eyes and think of them all bright and shining with light. Then an angel comes down because he can see where they are. He wraps them up in a beautiful white scarf that has stars all over it, and takes them up to Heaven. So, when we look up at the sky tonight, there will be a bright new star." She stopped for a moment and thought very hard. The dog took the opportunity to give her face a quick lick.

"So we don't have to cry any more. Stars dance and twinkle *on account of* they're wagging their tails and barking."

I snapped back to the present, to the bare room with the white walls. I looked at the man. He didn't speak.

"Why do you think Christ wore red? I mean you'd expect white, wouldn't you? But red...red is the colour of blood. It's vibrant and joyful too. It's the colour of flamenco dancers' dresses."

In the silence that followed, fragments of thoughts and feelings began to merge.

"I would like to have stayed on the mountain top. Why did I have to come back?"

I tried to take a deep breath. I struggled to draw it through the blocked place around my heart. I gasped and choked as I strained to reach a higher pitch. The air hopscotched painfully over the obstructions. My body shuddered. My lungs swelled to bursting point. Quite suddenly, the last piece of the jigsaw slotted into place, and a suspended chord resolved with a sigh.

How could I have been so stupid? How could I have been so very stupid? I had to come back. Of course I had to come back. I had to come back because there was something I had left undone.

CHAPTER TWENTY-SEVEN

25 March

So that's what it was all about. At last I understand. Driven by powerful anger at someone or something, you slammed down the final curtain. You hoped that would end it all. You forfeited your body, the vehicle that carried you down the winding lanes of your short journey through life. You took a chance and lost.

Too late, you discovered that death is more than the cold burn of a last ignored kiss. It's more than the tolling of a lonely bell, or the scrape of shovels on stone. Death is more than the dull thud of earth on wood.

You shuffled off the mortal coil, but in that sleep of death, you discovered that the fire of thought burned bright. Your mind survived, your spirit remained. Still earthbound, you became a vibration without a body, a song without words. Without a body you had no flute on which to pipe your tune.

I tuned in to your frequency, picked up your distress signal, but I couldn't decipher your message.

You remained trapped. You needed help. Despairing,

your thoughts reached out to me. But I myself was trapped. Force-fed on religion, confused, I too thought that death was the end.

Our thoughts intertwined. Terrified of death and the manner of your death, mine held you firmly attached to the earth. Desperate to communicate your discovery, yours pushed me beyond the boundaries. You haunted my weakness, snared my shortcomings. You confronted me with my omissions.

Locked in mutual obsession, we straddled the dividing line between the worlds. Unable to rest, we paced up and down, one feeding off the other. Determined, you goaded me, spurred me on. Furious at my stupidity, you pushed me down the stairs.

You dragged me unprepared through a land of dark shadows and earthbound spirits, a dangerous journey with only my own fears and prejudices to keep me company.

I had no sword, no Excalibur to protect me. You gave me no winged sandals, no Cap of Darkness, such as Athena gave to Perseus. No fairy godmother appeared and waved her wand. I was Cinderella without a ballgown. Only the rats gnawed at the edge of my consciousness.

Clues signposted the journey.

Music held the answer but I had strangled the child of nature in my labour for logic. I used music as a fortress against childhood fears, a barrier against trauma, a buffer against life. It swirled around me, hinted at secrets, free, as it dipped and soared. It defied all boundaries. It sang to my soul, "Listen, listen, there's more."

The dogged dream jogged my memory. When I closed my eyes to sleep, it kept my heart awake. It played and replayed. All night long, it whispered, "Search, search, there's more."

And so, my merciless catalyst, my shadow, you slipped past my guard. You stormed the sealed chamber of my living tomb. You persevered. When you had prepared the ground, the dream startled me out of my stupor.

ii

And now it's over. At last it's over.

I eat. I close my eyes at night and slip into uninterrupted sleep. Like a hostage taken prisoner in a strange land, blindfolded, buried underground, I lived only through my own tortured thoughts.

Eyes accustomed to darkness look at the light of the sun. Amazement replaces fear. In my absence the world seems to have been spring-cleaned.

Dazzled, I shade my eyes from skies graded in blues from stonewashed morning to lapis lazuli, cobalt and indigo.

I examine the forest green of holly, the emerald grass and the cool green of a grasshopper who seems to have been marinated in Chartreuse.

As sleepy spring awakes and stretches, every bud and blossom, every chirp from a newly built or recycled nest finds an echo in me. I touch the furry underside of a leaf, stroke pussy willow with the back of my fingers, close my hands over soft clumps of cool primroses.

iii

Dublin

I never thought I would know a day like today. Yet as I lie here under the sloping ceiling, everything looks the same.

The rain that beats against the window pane is the same rain. The chorus of dogs sounds the same. The black dog, the cantor, intones the first snarls and growls. The regular quintet of two assertive baritones, one tenor whose bark breaks with enthusiasm, and two hysterical counter tenors, replies.

But I feel different. I feel like a newborn child. Although there are no parents present to croon a lullaby, I feel protected, a grace-note in the divine symphony.

Flashes of blue-black and chestnut flit past the bedroom window. The swallows are back. They pause and ride on currents of air. They swoop and scud in graceful flight.

A tiny wren with a tip-tilted tail balances on a song-post. He pours out his heart in a joyous cadenza. The penetrating and jubilant trills of his clear sweet song encircle the Heavens and the earth.

The picture over the fireplace watches as I move through the house. The expression in the eyes has softened.

Dear Mr Shaw, you knew all along.

I cup my hands over my face.

My nostrils fill, my lungs swell with the fragrance of forests and mountains. It carries me away, far away from the world of brown envelopes, of bankers and solicitors, of limitation and pain, of ignorance and lack of love, a world in which we forget that stars glimmer even though we cannot always see them.

It carries me past monsters and creatures who crawled from the deep, back to the first sound, to the beginning that always was and always will be.

So here we are, two violins placed side by side, battle-scarred from painful tuning, battle-fatigued from the wrench of the pegs to tauten the slack strings.

The Unseen Hand plucks a string. We both vibrate in sympathy. Out of a still pool, a melody begins. Larger and larger hoops encircle the fine vibration.

You've taught me that an instrument's purpose is to make music. One is useless without the other. The sweep of the bow brings the strings to life. The hidden melody bridges the gap between Heaven and earth.

Thanks to you, I dare to step outside the high safe walls, dare to make my soft sound, dare shyly to join in the harmony that resonates with the universe.

So let us applaud. The play is over.

iv

And now the time has come for us to part, time to set one another free. You must go, your life transposed into another key, and I must stay, my life enriched by your priceless gift.

I release you to continue your soul's journey, back to that first vibration of truth, of music and love. I release you to return to the First Breath, the Sigh that makes the wind blow, the birds sing and the saplings grow.

So fly away and let my life sing.